“It’s okay. I’ve got you. In through the nose, doctor. Out through the mouth. Focus on me. Look at me.”

Jackson had sensed it, the looming panic attack. Moving closer, he ran his hands down Lucy’s arms one more time. Reached for the shaking hand in her lap.

“I’m here, Luce,” he said softly, the breath pushed out from his words whispering over her skin as he kissed the back of her hand. “I’m not going anywhere, ever. Okay?”

She looked back at Jackson, and the strength of conviction in his expression almost felled her. As though the swirling brown of his eyes was more intensive, boring into her soul to bring the words home.

“You believe me, right? Luce?”

She nodded, squeezing his hand tight with her own. “I know you’ll stay with me.”

“Forever, Lucy. You’ll never be alone again. Not while I’m here,” he rumbled, pulling their entwined hands to rest against his chest.

Dear Reader,

Book seven—how did that happen?

I loved dreaming up this story—the core of this idea has been in my head for a long time. As ever, my editor Soraya and Harlequin believed in the tale and helped me to shape it to be the very best book for you all to enjoy. As ever, I wouldn't be able to write these stories without my readers, so thank you all!

I sincerely hope you love reading this book and enjoy escaping from the real world, if only for a few hours.

Happy reading!

Rachel Dove

A BABY TO CHANGE THEIR LIVES

RACHEL DOVE

ISBN-13: 978-1-335-59551-5

A Baby to Change Their Lives

For questions and comments about the quality of this book, please contact us at CustomerService@Harlequin.com.

Harlequin Enterprises ULC
22 Adelaide St. West, 41st Floor
Toronto, Ontario M5H 4E3, Canada
www.Harlequin.com

Printed in U.S.A.

Rachel Dove is a writer and teacher living in West Yorkshire with her husband, their two sons and their animals. In July 2015, she won the *Prima* magazine and Mills & Boon Flirty Fiction Competition. She was the winner of the Writers Bureau Writer of the Year Award in 2016. She has had work published in the UK and overseas in various magazines and newspaper publications.

Books by Rachel Dove

Harlequin Medical Romance

Fighting for the Trauma Doc's Heart
The Paramedic's Secret Son
Falling for the Village Vet
Single Mom's Mistletoe Kiss
A Midwife, Her Best Friend, Their Family
How to Resist Your Rival

Visit the Author Profile page at Harlequin.com.

In honor of the late, great and much-loved

Eric Bell

Praise for
Rachel Dove

"I found Rachel Dove's interpretation broke that mold and I enjoyed the realistic way in which she painted the personalities. All in all, the well-crafted characters plus the engaging story had me emotionally invested from the start. Looking forward to reading more of Rachel's work."

—*Goodreads* on *Fighting for the Trauma Doc's Heart*

CHAPTER ONE

THE IRONY OF meeting her work nemesis on an NHS 'team-building' day was not lost on Lucy Bakewell. She didn't want to be here in the first place and, given what she had just endured, she knew her gut, as ever, had been right on the money. She didn't 'do' people at the best of times, and enforced bonding such as this set her teeth on edge. The last hour had been particularly abysmal: mud, testosterone, stupid, cumbersome apparel and bullets pinging past her ears. It was her worst nightmare.

Well, it was right up there, anyway. Definitely top three, and she was no shrinking violet either. Lucy was used to high pressure situations—at work she thrived in them—but this? This was her idea of pure unadulterated torture, all in the great outdoors. What was even worse than the last hour was her current situation. She was doing something that she'd never thought she would in a million years. Instead of being at work, doing what she loved, she was here, *hiding*, sheepishly hanging out in the huts that masqueraded as toilets, praying for a miracle to get her out of there.

Just as she was wiping the last bit of thick mud off her face, there was a loud barrage of knocking at the door.

'Are you still in there, or did you fall down the pan?' *No way.* She knew that voice. She'd just listened to it howl in pain.

'Er...yeah! Still here.'

Worst luck.

She eyed the toilet bowl. If she'd thought she could crawl her way out Andy Dufresne style, she'd already have been long gone. 'I'll be right out!'

She used the last bit of toilet roll in the stall at least to try to look clean before reluctantly sliding back the lock and facing her aggressor. He didn't look amused.

'I wondered if you were in there trying to fake some kind of emergency.'

'Of course not,' she lied. 'Just...freshening up. What is it that you want, exactly?'

He frowned, leaning closer and plucking a glob of mud from her pinned-back light-blonde hair. The masked helmet thing they'd made them wear had destroyed her usual neat and functional look—another reason to detest the day. The guy in front of her looked right at home. He didn't look ruffled, which made her feel even worse.

'Yeah?' His voice was deep, masculine. The kind of voice that you took notice of. 'No mirror in there, I'm guessing?' He looked amused. She could tell he was suppressing a grin. His twitching lips gave him away. 'I just wanted to see if you were coming. They're waiting to start the next game.'

Dear Lord in heaven, I'd rather deal with an outbreak of diarrhoea and vomiting on my ward than play again.

She focused on keeping the look of pure revulsion from breaking out across her rather sweaty face. 'Oh, that's fine. I can sit it out.'

He was already moving her away from the hut back to the paint-balling area.

'Not a chance. All participation is compulsory, remember?' She did remember.

All department heads are to attend. Cover has already been arranged.

It was so annoying. Also, it wasn't true. Her future brother-in-law Ronnie wasn't here as Head of A&E! She was still salty about that too. Sure, he was only Acting Head, but he was a sure thing for the job. He'd been filling in for two months since the department head had left. He should have been here, if only to endure this so-called morale booster with her.

She didn't need a morale boost, she needed real funding for her department. She needed her nurses and support staff to get paid a decent wage so she could keep them on her team and not lose them to better paid private sector positions. What was running around in a muddy field in the middle of a chilly February going to achieve?

'Anyway,' her adversary continued, unaware of her snarky inner monologue, 'After the last game, I have a score to settle, Lucky Shot.' He pointed to his long, camo-clad legs where a very noticeable and brightly coloured paintball splat was glaring up from his crotch area. Lucy winced; he had her there, not that she'd ever let him know it.

She puffed up her indignation instead. 'I did apologise for that.' She huffed. 'And you didn't have to be such a baby about it. It's not like we're using live ammo, and I've never done this before. I'm not exactly the gun-toting type.'

'Yeah, more Calamity Jane than GI Jane, eh?' he scoffed, making her scowl deepen.

Having her flaws pointed out by anyone was not something she relished, never mind from a stranger who she'd almost maimed.

'You hit that neurosurgeon guy pretty hard in the coccyx,' he banged on, frog-marching her back to her fate. 'He's been icing his backside for the last ten minutes.'

They were almost back at the starting point, and Lucy's anxiety was growing with every step. She could see the other medical professionals all looking around, some brandishing paint guns as though they were extras in an action movie. A couple of them were eyeing her warily. Normally, she would have revelled in the fear she had produced. Today, she felt as if she might end up on the evening news for shooting an ear off a consultant or something. It did nothing to soothe her frazzled nerves, and if there was one thing on this planet Lucy hated it was the feeling of not being in total control.

'Well,' she retorted sulkily, tutting when her jailer jumped away from the business end of the weapon she was waving. 'Why did we need to do this anyway? I barely get time off from the hospital as it is, and now I have to spend an entire day off shooting at other stressed out department heads? I mean, who's running the hospitals while we're all here playing "shoot them up"?'

He chuckled at the side of her, pushing her gun down to aim at the floor as they walked. When she glanced his way, she could see he was almost…smiling. His groin and pride were obviously recovering. He looked as if he belonged here, dressed like a soldier in the woods. He was tall, dark, handsome and rugged with a five o'clock shadow that made him look as if he'd slept rough under the stars after a day wrangling wild horses.

He was different from the other, weedier men on the field today—almost too alpha male to be some department head in some hospital somewhere. Most of the doctors she'd encountered over the years were like Ronnie—softer; geeky, almost—less Bear Grylls and more teddy bear.

Most of them considered golfing a serious sport. This guy, in comparison, looked gruffer than that. He was wood-chopping burly. He probably loved these activities or even did them for fun.

He was kind of cute, she noticed reluctantly. If she ever decided to have a dating life other than a few scattered first dates, he would probably be her type. Not that she'd taken the time to consider what her type was beyond the odd passing thought.

'I mean, look at them all. Hardly the A-Team, are we?'

'Why don't you say what you really think?' he joked, his laugh deep, rich. Stopping short of meeting the others, he came to stand in front of her. 'I'm Jackson, by the way.'

He flashed her a smile that on impact disarmed any remaining snarkiness she felt. Sure, he'd not reacted in the best way to her assault, calling her a 'ridiculous woman', but she'd never been shot in the crown jewels. She decided to let it pass. Maybe her day would be tolerable after all.

'Lucy—Head of Paediatrics at Leeds General.' She shook the huge hand he held out, feeling it dwarf hers entirely.

He shot her one of those smiles again. It made the dimples in his cheeks stand out. Lucy had to look at her feet to stop herself from fawning over him. If her work colleagues back home saw her like this, she would never live it down. Being a ballbuster was something she prided herself on. 'Well, hello, Lucy! It's so weird I met you today, I'm actually—'

'Come on, you two!' The over-enthusiastic paintball instructor, who was ironically named Tag, came and shuffled them both over to the waiting teams. Lucy was on the red team, Jackson on the blue. 'Game two commences in two minutes! Get your masks back on, make sure your guns are reloaded.' He stared pointedly at Lucy. 'And remember, it's the torso you are aiming for. No below the belt shots. Team building, remember?'

Lucy shot him a sarcastic grin, thrusting her mask over her face to stop her from biting back with a retort. She was pretty sure she heard a rumbling laugh from Jackson's direction.

'Positions, people! Let's have some fun!'

Lucy's groan was drowned out by the others' loud whoops.

The second game was even worse. Released from their usual whitewashed, walled workplaces, and possibly hungry for lunch, the medical professionals were unrecognisable from their usual polished and pedantic selves. The second the whistle went, it was all out war between the reds and the blues.

'Let's do this!' one of the red women bellowed. 'For the win!'

'Come on, now!' Lucy tried to placate the baying masses. 'It's just a game!'

'I am not going back labelled a loser! Reds, we win this—we win or die!'

'Slightly dramatic,' Lucy countered, but someone shoved past her and she ended up knee-deep in the mud. 'Hey!' she yelled, her surprise turning to anger when she saw who'd pushed her.

'Blue team, with me!' Jackson growled, taking off for the tree line like some kind of Viking warrior. He turned to look at her when she shouted his name, and she was waiting for him to say sorry when he kept running and raised his gun, pointing it at her breast plate. 'Take the red scum down! Death to the reds!'

Lucy heard the pings and splats of his paintballs sail past as she rolled away. Jumping to her feet, she grappled for the gun slung from her waist.

Okay, now it's on, jerk.

'Reds!' she yelled. 'Get it together!'

A short bloke with a red sash ran to her side. 'We're outnumbered! We're never going to make it!'

Lucy grabbed his jacket as he babbled about targets and something about not being made for violence. 'Shut up and fire at something!' she chided, half-dragging him to the tree line further down. Their flag was in the hut near where Jackson had run, and she just knew he was going to try to get the win. Which would not only mean he would equalise, with her scrotum shot having secured their first win by slowing him down, but even worse than defeat it would go to best out of three. Which would mean another game with these hungry, half-crazed knuckleheads. It was getting very *Lord of the Flies*, and she wasn't about to endure this a third time. 'We can't lose this one!'

The man, an ENT specialist from somewhere in Scotland, whimpered as they made the trees and sank to the floor, out of sight. 'We only won the last one because you took out the sasquatch! We have no hope now; he'll be at the hut by now! Emmett won't be able to hold him off; he's only an orthopaedic surgeon, not Rambo!'

Lucy bit her lip. 'Seriously, this is the NHS's finest? We faced Covid, and the government dropping us right in it, and one big dude with a cheeky smile and a gung-ho attitude is enough to terrify you all?'

The woman who'd hollered earlier crawled across from the nearest crop of trees commando-style. 'Basically, yes. I told management that this would suck. I suggested a spa day…'

She suddenly stood up, firing off a volley of shots and punching the air when she heard a satisfying yelp from a distance.

'Yes! Got one!'

'Nice!' Lucy cheered, picking up on the woman's Scottish accent. Pointing at her quivering tree mate, she motioned to the woman. 'I'm Lucy. He one of yours?'

'John? Yeah. I'm Annie. Do you think he breached the hut yet? That Emmett dude is on his own up there. Bigfoot will snap him like a twig.'

Hmm; it seemed Jackson had made an impression on everyone, not just her. She rather liked his height…

What? Concentrate! He's the enemy.

If he got that flag, lunch would be even further away, which would mean more of this torture. Looking at John, who was now hugging the tree and reciting anatomically correct body parts like a mantra as the blues hollered in the distance, she knew they were never going to make it.

'I'll try to take him out before he gets to the flag,' she whispered, pointing to the break in the line of trees where their hut stood. 'Make sure our team goes for theirs. Cover me, okay?'

'God speed,' John urged, releasing the tree to hug her and take up position, gun aimed. 'Annie, watch my six!'

Annie was already picking off another blue player who'd popped up at the wrong time.

'Go, Lucy, now! I'll go for the blue flag!'

Lucy closed her eyes, took a deep breath and ran as fast as she could for the hut. 'Thank God I love the treadmill,' she huffed to herself, ducking as a blue player popped up from behind a bush and nearly took off her head. Springing back up, she popped a shot at his leg.

'Ow! I'm out!' he yelped, before slinking off towards the refreshments tent, his gun trailing along behind. Lucy didn't wait to see who he was talking to, nor to see what had happened to make John scream behind her like a banshee behind her. She had one goal: to take Jackson out. Annie was right: he was the real enemy on that team; the others were just following his lead. They would be no match for Annie. Lucy had a feeling she worked in microsurgery or radiology or something, judging by her crack shot. She'd ask her over lunch, she decided, spying the hut with a grin, when they were enjoying their winning feast.

She stopped by the closest barrier, a wooden fence covered in burlap and curved around the edge of the red hut. It was quiet—a little too quiet.

'Emmett?' she called out. Nothing. 'Emmett?'

Still nothing. He wasn't there yet! If Jackson had taken Emmett out, the game would be over. The blue team would be crowing over the rest of them for sure.

The background shots sped up. Annie was going for it, by the sounds of it. Lucy could hear the blues shouting to each other, 'Take her out!' When she heard a string of profanity in a thick Scottish accent, she knew that her number two was holding her own. She saw another barrier nearer the red hut and decided to move position.

The lack of blues heading for their red flag told her that they had a plan, and Jackson was no doubt near, waiting to pounce.

Before her foot hit the floor, she heard it—the snap of a tree root a few metres away. Ducking down, her eyes narrowing beneath the mask, she saw him. Even bent over at the other side of the opposite barrier, he was bigger than her, more noticeable. She waited for him to turn the gun on her, but his aim stayed focused on the hut. He hadn't seen her. She reached for her gun, aware of every little movement of her clothing, the placement of her feet on the forest floor. Even her breath, which was coming out in shallow, excited bursts of adrenaline, filled air.

'Lucy.' She jumped at the sound of her name being called out. 'You got some explaining to do! Where are you? You know the aim of the game is to get the opponent's flag, right?'

She had to bite down hard on her lip to avoid the retort she wanted to throw back at him. *Smug git.* He knew she was there and was trying to get into her head.

Nice try...wrong woman.

'Lucy!' he sang out again. The competitor in her was well and truly fired up by this Neanderthal. He'd really got under her skin for some reason. She wasn't used to it, and the fact he was good-looking was a distraction.

Behind them, a volley of shots rang out, raised

voices bouncing off the trees around them. Lucy couldn't make out the voices. She hoped it wasn't Annie getting taken down.

'Sounds like your team to me,' Jackson teased. 'Best of three, eh, Lucky Shot?'

Not on your life, she fumed inwardly.

She focused back on him, just in time to see him move from behind his cover. *Now or never*, she realised. *This is for lunch. For the red team. For women doctors everywhere.*

Holding in a jagged breath, she closed one eye, focused on the trigger and squeezed.

Pop-pop-pop!

'What the…? Son of a— Ow!'

She scrunched down tight as he came into the clearing with a jump, holding his backside. He pulled off his mask, his head scanning the terrain, and she could see the anger in his expression. 'Lucy! Where are you?'

She stood up, waggling her gloved fingers in his direction.

'Right here, my favourite yeti. I win again, it seems.'

'You didn't win! You shot me in the butt—what do you mean, "yeti"?'

The siren rang out in the distance. Lucy saw Jackson's scowl deepen, and she saw why when she followed his gaze. A huge plume of red smoke was floating above the trees. Turning back to him, pulling off her own mask and letting her blonde hair fly free, she grinned triumphantly. He was glaring at her, rubbing at a spot on his rump.

'Like I said, we win.'

She could hear the others laughing and celebrating a short distance away, and she turned to join them. She was already looking forward to her spoils—a good lunch and an early shower after this enforced activity day.

She was almost out of ear shot when Jackson's words stopped her in her tracks.

'I was telling you something earlier when we got interrupted.'

'Yeah,' she called out, not bothering to turn around.

'Yeah,' he half-growled back. 'I was telling you that I'm the new A&E department head.'

Turning on her heel, she looked him dead in the eye. It was intoxicating, all this winning. She felt as if she could take on the world right then. He was still rubbing at his backside, and she pushed away the pang of remorse she felt at shooting the man yet again—the first cute man she'd seen in a long time too, worse luck. Good job she didn't have time for all that romance anyway. Somehow, work always got in the way somehow or the other. Even winning today had become a bit of an obsession, she realised.

'Congratulations on the job,' she told him earnestly. 'Perhaps your new staff can patch you up when you get back. Just don't tell them a little bitty woman did it, eh?' She bit at her lip, realising she could be a little nicer in victory; Harriet, her sister, was always telling her that. 'Listen, it's just a game. I got carried away, you were being smug… Let's go get some—'

'Smug? You shot me—twice—in two very painful places! I know your type; you have to win, don't you, have to come on top? Seriously, you didn't even want to play the game!'

'Says you! You were acting like the SAS, all testosterone and macho pecs.'

'Macho pecs? Who do you think you are?'

'I think I know your type. Your fragile male ego can't take being outsmarted, with your big old manly chin, and your growly voice. It's paintballing, not war.'

'Oh, yeah, it is.' He snorted. 'You taking a shot at my posterior saw to that. We'll be seeing each other again, so it looks like you'll be seeing my *manly pecs* on a regular basis.'

Lucy rolled her eyes. 'I'm sure we can survive lunch without killing each other.'

'I don't mean that.' He laughed softly. 'A&E at your hospital, Lucy.' He half-limped over to her. 'I'm starting at Leeds General on Monday.'

She felt her jaw drop. 'My hospital?'

This time, it was Jackson doing the grinning. 'Yep. You're looking at the new Head of A&E.'

'I didn't know,' she admitted, her eyes wide with realisation.

‘Yeah, well, that was obvious.’

‘I thought Ronnie would get the job.’ She said this half to herself, thinking about her sister’s husband. She knew he’d gone for the job.

Another reason to hate this dude.

‘So I don’t deserve the job?’

‘Well, no, but Ronnie is already there—part of the team.’

‘I interviewed fair and square. Take it up with HR if you don’t like it.’ He folded his thick arms against his chest, still bristling with anger. ‘It was Ronnie who told me about the job in the first place, if you must know.’

‘You know Ronnie?’

He laughed. ‘You could say that, yeah. I thought he was joking about you, but I can see now he underplayed his description.’

What? Ronnie had told this jackass about her? Why was he telling people about her?

Her defences were well and truly up now. She’d been up for flirting with this guy, and he’d already known who she was. She didn’t like it. ‘Yeah,’ she countered. ‘Well, Ronnie said nothing about you, and my world was better for it.’

She couldn’t help but smirk, seeing him pout. He raised a dark brow when he saw her mocking expression. His eyes flashed bright, which made her smirk all the more. It was quite fun, sparring with him. At work, people tended to just do as she asked. She wasn't mean, but her need for perfection and absorption in her job often made her come across as curt, aloof. It was kind of nice to butt heads with someone. 'Don't pout, Jackie boy. With shoulders as big as those, I would have thought you could carry an insult a little better.'

He huffed out a laugh. 'Yeah, well, with little sparrow legs like yours, I would have thought you would be used to running to keep up with the crowd.' They both stood there, lips twitching with the need to suppress their laughter. She was enjoying this, but so was he, she realised when he grinned back at her wolfishly.

What is going on here? Why hadn't Ronnie told her about this guy, about him being here today? Was her sister matchmaking again?

'Yeah, well, good things come in small packages. I could run rings around you any day of the week. Don't think that I'll give you an easy ride when you come to General.' She fixed him with her sternest gaze. 'We don't play games at work, and if you got the job over Ronnie, well, you had better earn it.' Family was important to her, something to be protected. They didn't need a fox in their hen house, disturbing things, ruffling feathers. When was change ever good, other than in medicine?

'Earn it, eh?' His playful look was long gone now. He was closed off. She might have mourned it if she hadn't been so guarded. 'Well, time will tell, little lady.' He side-stepped her on his way to meet the others. 'I'm Ronnie's brother, by the way—Jackson Denning. I'm sure he mentioned me.'

Lucy almost fainted on the spot.

His brother? Oh, my God.

It clicked. Ronnie's older brother, Jackson, was a doctor, working overseas. Harriet had babbled on about him moving back to the UK. As usual, Lucy hadn't listened. 'You're…' She was stumbling over her own tongue now. 'You're his brother, Jackson.'

It was his turn to smirk now. He'd turned around and she could see it now—the Denning jawline, the chocolate hue of his eyes. 'Didn't I just say that?' The fact he was still nursing his bottom while pinning her with his gaze made her face flush for more reasons than one. 'See you at work. Enjoy the rest of your weekend, Trigger.'

He waggled his fingers behind him as if he was pressing a gun trigger, and for the first time in her life Lucy understood what people meant when they said their blood was boiling. Something about the big idiot currently walking away from her made her want to grind her teeth down to stumps.

'You're being childish,' she called after him. 'I didn't know who you were!'

'"You're being childish",' he mocked back in a squeaky voice. 'Be seeing ya, Lucy. Real soon.'

He disappeared out of sight, and she stood alone in the forest.

'Hell,' she muttered to herself. 'Well, you've done it now, Bakewell.'

She started her slow trudge towards camp. Ronnie and Harriet were going to have a field day when they heard.

CHAPTER TWO

Five years later

'HARRIET, YOU KNOW I'll try.'

Lucy allowed her forehead to rest against the large glass window for a moment, listening to her little sister's trademark slow sigh. The one that told Lucy in no uncertain terms that her sister was disappointed. She'd been doing it since they'd been fresh-faced teenagers, taking very different paths despite there only being a couple of years between the pair.

'I know,' Harriet said down the line. 'I get it. I just wanted you there. You know it's just us.'

Lucy lifted her head when a nurse came to check a patient history with her. 'Just a sec, Harry.

'Yes,' she agreed with the nurse. 'Monitor her every hour and call the parents to update them. I sent them down to get something to eat while the tests were being done.' The nurse nodded, leaving Lucy alone again in front of the viewing window of the SCBU—Lucy's little haven, where she came to remind herself why she did the job in the first place. Why she was probably going to miss her niece's second birthday, and why she was currently getting the sigh from her younger sibling. To remind herself why she annoyed her family with the sacrifices she made again and again.

'I'm back, Harriet, but I have to get back to the ward. And you are not allowed to play the "dead parents" card—no other family guilt trip for another month at least. I promise, I will try my best to get there. I already changed my shift, but you know what it's like.'

But Harriet didn't, not really. She'd been a teaching assistant before having Zoe; now she was a full-time mum. She'd never been one for all-consuming careers and motherhood together. She was happy to have taken a few years off to raise Zoe full-time. She'd wanted family more than anything else, and now she was a mother herself—a great mum; the kind who used Pinterest and made handmade gifts and elaborate cupcakes every Christmas. The polar opposite of Lucy, who was a workaholic with half a cucumber and a bottle of vodka in her fridge as opposed to real food.

When their parents had passed away when they'd been younger, Lucy only just an adult, they'd both veered off in different directions. Lucy had devoted herself to medicine and looking after her teenage sister, and Harriet had grown up wanting family life more than ever. The one thing they had in common though, was their fierce love for each other. Trauma was a pretty strong glue, and it held people together.

'Well, Jackson's coming; he took the day off.'

Lucy turned to look back at the special care babies, feeling her irritation grow tenfold at the mention of Dr Perfect. She scowled at the floor, wishing he could feel her scorn through the layers of brick. Being an A&E doctor was hard—and, sure, running a department was hardly a doddle; she could attest to that herself. But still, did he have to make her feel like an idiot in front of her sister?

His Mr Wonderful routine over the last few years had really got on her nerves, if she was honest. He still insisted on calling her Trigger, which made her want to peel off her own skin. He pulled faces at her like a petulant toddler whenever she alone was looking, and he seemed to revel in the fact that he irritated the ever-living hell out of her just by existing in the same proximity. Sure, she did the same to him, but still—he was the jerk in this situation. Sometimes she even wished for a paintball gun, just so she could pop one off again. That day had set the tempo of their working relationship. They were like stagnant embers around each other, fired into life by the other's presence. Every time she crossed paths with him at the hospital, she had to consciously work on not strangling him with her stethoscope.

To make matters worse, he was liked by everyone else. Of all the people to be her sister's brother-in-law, of course it had to be the flashy doc who loved to wind her up at every opportunity. The one guy she secretly fancied even while he was the biggest pain in her butt.

They'd become family after that day. She'd been maid of honour at Ronnie's and Harriet's wedding and he'd been the best man. He was there every time they did something as a family. Family holidays were quite often torture, with Jackson in his bathing shorts, tanned and beautiful, being ogled by women around the pool, while Lucy stuck her head in a book and slathered herself in suntan lotion.

She knew he at her looked too; she could see him run his eyes over her sometimes. He'd make little comments about a new dress. He always seemed to notice when she had her hair cut or did something new with it. It had been five years of tension between them, sexual and otherwise, and it showed no sign of stopping. But he was family, her sister's brother-in-law, uncle to her niece, so she did what she usually did—she buried it. Focused on the fact that, despite the fact he made her pulse quicken, he also well and truly got on her wick.

'Yeah, well, he would.'

Of course Jackson was going. He never put a foot wrong, did he? *Jackass.* Whenever he worked late and missed a family occasion, he was given a free pass by her own sister.

'What was that?' Harriet said down the phone line.

'Nothing,' Lucy half-sang back. 'Listen, I have to go, but I'll see you there, okay?'

'Fine.' Harriet breathed. 'Love you, sis.'

'Love you too.' Lucy smiled back. 'Give Zoe a big hug from her favourite aunt.'

'You're her only aunt.' Harriet laughed. 'I will. See you soon.'

Lucy glanced at the time on her phone before going back to paediatrics. If she was going to try and get to that birthday party, she had to get going.

'Cute, aren't they?'

Jackson took in the little sleeping bundle in the back of his brother's car. Her hair was stuck up in little tufts, and she was sweaty from the afternoon's exertions. She was adorable.

'Yeah, but I couldn't eat a whole one.'

Ronnie chuckled, wiping a stray blob of chocolate off his daughter's cheek. She stirred, her eyelashes fluttering, before her head dropped again.

'You're the worst, you know that, right?'

'Of course. That's why I don't procreate like you.' Jackson leaned in, brushing Zoe's little warm hand. 'She is all your wife, though, right down to those baby blues.'

Ronnie wasn't offended in the slightest. 'I know.

Good genes.' Jackson watched his little brother's contented grin turn devilish. The pair of them were standing by Ronnie's car in the car park of the local soft play area where they'd just partied. Well, if he could call ten very enthusiastic toddlers screeching and whooping for two hours on a sugar high partying.

'Speaking of genes, here comes Auntie Lucy!'

Jackson's lip curled into a smile before he could stop himself, seeing Lucy turn into the car park. She practically screeched to a stop a few spaces away. Seconds later, the door was flung open to a chorus of, 'Sorry, sorry! I had an emergency at the last minute I couldn't hand off!'

Jackson watched her face fall when she took in the scene, Zoe tuckered out and sound asleep.

'Oh, no! I missed the whole thing? Really?'

She scooped a huge cellophane-trimmed basket from the back seat and huffed her way over. Jackson saw the tension in her shoulders; she was wrapped up tighter than the over-the-top birthday gift.

'Sis, I told you not to go mad!' Ronnie, as ever, was thrilled to see his sister-in-law, who looked like his pretty blonde wife. They had the same hair colour and cute little brows sitting over bright blue-green eyes.

That was where the similarities ended, however. Harriet was always calm, collected. The twisted-up pretzel stomping over to them was someone who played a whole different ball game. Even at a kid's party, her face looked pinched. Her eyes roved over the party goers leaving with their progeny, who were all either half-asleep in their parents' arms or still bouncing up and down from their cake and fun overload. Jackson watched her watching them and wondered what was going on in that pretty head of hers. It was kind of a hobby of his, working her out.

Ronnie took the gift basket from her, his eyes boggling at the array of clothes and toys stuffed into the gift. 'This is ridiculous. She's only two, you know, not leaving for uni with the need for a capsule wardrobe. Did you leave anything in the shop?'

She rolled her eyes with a good-natured smirk, and Jackson watched silently as her shoulders started to dip.

'Well, I don't see her as much as I'd like. I have to spoil my only niece, right?' The furrow between her brows returned with a vengeance when she spotted her in the back seat. 'She's asleep.' She looked…disappointed. Jackson could see it written all over her face, just before she hid it behind the expression he was most accustomed to seeing—that of the closed-up professional. The expression that had given her the nickname Medusa at work. Not that anyone dared say it in her proximity; that would be professional suicide. If her glare didn't turn them to stone first, her tongue lashings were strong enough to strip the hide from a rhino.

Personally, he preferred his pet name for her, Trigger. It suited her better. She even answered to it sometimes, when she wasn't thinking, which made it all the sweeter to Jackson. The fact it raised brows from the other terrified staff members cheered him up on the bad days. The irony of him watching her, figuring her out, while the rest of the hospital watched them never lost its sparkle. After working overseas in some of the hottest climates, their banter kept him warm. He couldn't help it. She got under her skin as much as he did hers. In different ways, he thought with a familiar pang that he brushed aside. She was family, and that was that.

'Yeah, sorry.' Ronnie winced. 'She wore herself out in there. She'll love waking up to this, though.' He dipped his head towards the huge gift.

'Yeah,' his sister-in-law murmured, the sadness weighing down her words. 'Sure. I'll just have to come and see her at the weekend—take her to the park or something. Where's my sister?'

Ronnie thumbed behind him. 'She's saying goodbye to the other nursery mums; you know what they are like when they get together.'

Jackson thought he saw another wince cross Lucy's features before she locked it back down under that prickly persona. She looked at him then, as though she'd only just realised he was there. Or, more likely, was only just deigning to acknowledge his presence.

'And I suppose you were here on time.'

Jackson held down the sarcastic smile he almost threw at her and kept it hidden. It would only inflame the fiery woman in front of him. Whilst he normally got a thrill out of it, especially at work, something about her expression made him hold back. He knew she was genuinely upset to have missed Zoe's party. Even he couldn't mock her for that; they both adored Zoe.

'I was. Day off.' He added unnecessarily, 'I'm not on call today either. Good result at work?'

'Tricky, but yeah.'

Jackson nodded back. 'I'm glad. Worth it, then.'

Her gaze slid back to Zoe, still tuckered out in the back seat. Her little blonde curls were ruffled from the breeze coming through the open door. Lucy didn't look too convinced. She was already chewing the inside of her cheek, a tell that she was working something out. He looked away when her eyes locked onto his. She stopped biting.

'Yeah, I guess. Well, I might as well go.' She didn't wait for her sister. She'd be mad, and they all silently acknowledged it. To Harriet, family was first over work, everything else in the world. That was one of the many ways the two women differed. Even being a doctor's wife hadn't softened Harriet on that. Work was the only thing that ever came between them. Jackson thought Harriet harsh at times, but of course he kept that to himself. Lucy wouldn't thank him for voicing it anyway, and he knew that Ronnie had never managed to get through to her on the topic. What Harriet didn't realise was, when they weren't home with Harriet and Zoe, they were saving other people's families. Allowing them to have more time together that otherwise they might never have had.

Ronnie put the gift away to give Lucy a goodbye hug. Jackson didn't step forward; they didn't hug. They clashed when she came down from her department in paediatric care and entered his realm in A&E. The nurses usually went running the second they started to lock horns.

Ronnie had even joked once that Jackson was Perseus. After witnessing one rather heated exchange in the stairwell, Ronnie had sent him a plastic sword and shield. He still had it above his desk at home. It made him laugh every time he saw it. Ronnie was definitely the referee between the two of them at work, and the glue that held the four of them together. He and Zoe, who'd been adored by all of them from the second they'd laid eyes on her.

'Well, thanks for coming. Harriet will understand. You know she just likes the family thing.'

Lucy's brows rose in line with the scepticism Jackson saw across her strained features.

'No, she won't.' Lucy smiled. It didn't meet her eyes, and Jackson busied himself with his phone as Lucy said goodbye to Ronnie, and said nothing as she pulled her car back onto the main road in the direction of her flat.

'Will Harriet really be that annoyed? I miss stuff; she never says anything to me.'

Ronnie shrugged. 'She tries to understand. She takes it different when Lucy's not there. She gets the job; I work enough hours myself. She just thinks differently. Losing their parents hardened one and softened the other.' Jackson had no need to ask which. 'They might be sisters, but DNA is about all they share. You know Harriet—she loves all this.' He waved a hand in the direction of the venue in which they'd just spent two eardrum-shattering hours. 'Lucy just wants different things. Harriet will be fine. I've got a babysitter for tomorrow night so I can take her out. You know, to celebrate the incoming terrible twos.'

Both men's eyes fell back on the sleeping baby nearby.

'I can't believe she's two already,' Jackson commented, marvelling as he always did at the tiny little person his brother had created. 'It doesn't seem like two minutes since you brought her home from the hospital.'

'I remember.' Ronnie laughed. 'It was the last day I got any sleep.'

'Ronnie!' Harriet appeared at the doorway, a bundle of gift bags hanging from her arms. 'Can I have a hand, love?'

Jackson took his leave. He was looking forward to the rest of his day off, away from the bustle of A&E. 'I'll let you get on. Have a good night tomorrow, okay? Send Harriet my love.'

Ronnie was already heading over to his wife, who was waddling towards him with the weight in her arms.

'Will do, bro. Pool next week?' he called out.

Jackson nodded with a grin. 'To take your money again? Try and stop me.'

He waited till the pair of them were heading back to their car before heading to his own, making sure Zoe wasn't alone. As he drove away, he saw Ronnie take the bags from his wife, encircling her in his arms. He looked away, focusing on the road ahead.

It would be nice to have that one day.

He pushed the thought away, not for the first time. He wasn't at that stage yet. He wasn't even dating, really. He hadn't met anyone he'd wanted to see beyond a couple of dates. He liked his easy life, working in a job he adored. He had the house, the car, financial stability. Sure, someone to sit on the couch with him would be great, but he couldn't really see what that would look like in real life. He didn't even have time for a pet, so how would he fit his life around a family? His thoughts turned to Lucy—her face when she'd realised she'd missed the party.

Maybe people just weren't meant to have everything they wanted.

He was doing fine on his own. The big life plan could wait, for now. There was no rush. He'd come home to put down roots after years of doctoring abroad, and he had plenty of time. In the past five years, he'd adjusted his expectations, that was all.

He headed home, looking forward to an afternoon of gym and rest. There was plenty of time for toddler parties and date nights, he told himself for the millionth time. He had family and friends; the rest could wait. Perhaps the pieces of his life didn't fit as he would like them to. But maybe it was enough that he had them in the first place.

CHAPTER THREE

The next day

JACKSON COULDN'T HELP but smirk as he heard the curtain swish back.

'You called for a consultation?'

'Yeah, I did.'

Lucy looked at the empty bed, her eyes narrowing as she looked at him standing there.

'Well, where's the patient? Triage One, you paged.'

'I put them in bed five—but Trig, wait!'

She'd already turned on her heel, but his hand whipped out to still her. He felt a zap of electricity pulse through him.

Huh; static of the uniform. Well, we are like repelling magnets.

Her aqua eyes widened, as though she'd felt it too, before they fell to see where his fingers had wrapped around the flesh of her forearm.

'Don't call me Trig,' she chided as his hand pulled away. 'What's wrong?'

'I needed to talk to you first. I think the child has pica.'

'Okay.' She nodded. 'What was the reason for attending today?'

'The little fella, Tom, aged five—he was helping his grandmother in the garden. Ate a bulb they were planting, or part of it.'

'Did you check whether it was toxic?'

Jackson nodded. 'Dahlia bulb; his grandmother acted pretty quickly. She got most of the bulb out of his mouth, and gave him water. No treatment needed this time, but it's his fourth admission in three months. The last time it was a Lego brick. He passed it without surgery, but I think he needs checking over—there could be more than pica at play here. He presents with some rigid behaviours, sensitivity to some sensory input… He doesn't speak very much, gives minimal eye contact. His mother's on the way; she was at work. The grandmother's pretty upset.'

He pursed his lips, remembering how the little guy's grandparent had wrung her hands together, her eyes never leaving the boy in the bed. Kids had that effect on people. He saw it time and time again. It was also one of the reasons he wasn't in the quickest rush to join the parenting brigade himself. Having that much worry and responsibility on top of running A&E seemed like a step too far—something he was reminded of by his patients from time to time.

'I bet she is, but from what you said she shouldn't blame herself. I remember a kid in my primary school class who used to eat sand. Children do the oddest things; they have no sense of danger. If pica is the diagnosis, it's a compulsion. Sounds like we might need to refer on to the neurodiversity pathway. I can speak to my team.' Lucy took the clipboard from him, her eyes scanning the paperwork. 'Thanks for the heads up. I'll go speak to the family. Have you mentioned your suspicions to them yet?'

Jackson stretched out his aching back with a wince. He'd been in resus before this case, working on a patient who'd had a heart attack in his front garden. He'd been one of the lucky ones, his next-door neighbour being a nurse who'd administered help quickly. The ambulance had blue-lighted him to the A&E doors, but he'd flatlined on the way in and the CPR had been tough. Jackson's back had started to sing during his stint, but he'd ignored it until the man was breathing and safe from the circling drain.

'Jackson? Earth to Dr Denning!'

'Sorry,' he apologised, shaking his head to wake himself up. 'And no, I figured I'd leave that to the Goddess of Paediatrics.' She rolled her eyes, but the usual fire and snark didn't come. He felt a little cheated. She'd been almost genial. Her game was off. Usually when he was feeling a little tired, or off *his* game, sparring with her fired him up and gave him an energy boost better than anything he could get from the vending machines around here. 'Come on, Trig—nothing? No comment back?'

She held the clipboard tight to her chest.

'Nope, I've got to get on. Busy day.'

He came to stand in front of her. 'Every day around here is a busy day. Really, what's up? You weren't right yesterday.'

'You noticed that, eh?'

He raised a brow. 'Spill. Patients are waiting.'

The sigh that rattled through her rib cage ruffled the papers she clutched to her chest.

'Fine, if it will shut you up. I feel like Harriet's mad at me. I rang her last night, and she was okay with me, but…'

'She judged you for not getting to the party?'

Her mouth lifted on one side, making her look oddly vulnerable.

'Yeah, I think so. She bites her tongue most of the time, but…' She bit her lip, and his eyes tracked the movement.

This is really getting to her.

'I didn't tell her the full truth, but we did have an emergency. I couldn't tell her how bad it was, of course, I never do. Perhaps if I had, she'd understand finally. I couldn't just leave to get to Zoe's party. Zoe was happy, healthy, eating cake with her friends. Sure, her auntie wasn't there, but would she have noticed really? She's two. She won't even remember the party, but if I said that to Harriet she'd explode!'

She was pacing around the cubicle, Jackson tracking her rant around the small curtained space, letting her get it out before they both went back to work. He rather liked these moments. When it was just the two of them, she was different, less guarded. She let him in. Not for the first time, he wondered what their working relationship might have been like if they'd met in different circumstances. If the dye of his character hadn't been set so firmly in her mind that day. If their families weren't entwined together.

'I…' She trailed off. 'Never mind.'

Jackson didn't want her to stop. 'Go on,' he said, his voice soft, low. 'Tell me.'

She pinned him to the spot with her baby blues, nibbling at her lip. He waited.

'Sometimes I wish she'd trained in medicine, like us, like Ronnie. I wish I could show her some of the horrors we see. The tiny coffins we work hard to avoid for our patients. You get it, and Ron does. Hell, A&E isn't all cuts and scrapes. She doesn't get it. I mean, our parents died in a horrific accident.'

She stopped walking, her free hand covering her heart as though saying the words had produced an ache. 'She remembers that; I mean, it's not something you'd ever forget, right? You'd think she'd be proud of us all, saving people. It's why I…'

The words fell away when her eyes met his

again. He could see the mental shields click back up into place in her mind. Huffing out a breath, she straightened the already collated papers in her hands. 'Anyway, I just feel a bit off today. I hate feeling at odds with her. She's my—'

'Family,' he finished for her. 'I get it.'

The pair stood across from each other, the hospital continuing on behind the curtain, noisy and full of life.

'Yeah.' She shrugged. 'Nothing will mess you up quite like blood relatives, eh?'

He laughed, and she looked surprised.

'Been a while since I made you laugh, eh?'

'Intentionally, yeah,' he agreed. 'I laugh *at* you all the time.'

'And we're back to normal. I'm glad. Heart to hearts aren't our thing, frenemy.' She tapped the board. 'I'll go see the patient now. See you later, Denning.'

Jackson was pretty sure that, before she left, Lucy had a smile on her face.

Hours later, he was still thinking about their talk. The emergency alert on his pager went off, jolting him from his thoughts. The second he got there, took in the scene. He wanted nothing but her—Lucy. He needed her here. She didn't know it yet, but their lives had just changed for ever. Even when the chaos had died down, he thought of that time in the cubicle. He wished that they could go back there. Wished he had said more. They could never go back to being those people, not now. The people they'e been in that moment were gone for ever.

CHAPTER FOUR

How is this happening? How did we get here?

The voice in Lucy's head wasn't as clear as normal. Her usual sharp mind felt as if it had been dipped in treacle, the cogs gummed up with the slush and debris of the last week and a half.

A week and a half. Ten measly days since she'd last been at work. Since her world had collapsed for the second time.

This was all she had now: a treacly brain, regrets and the welcoming, numbing feeling of shock and disbelief. It had taken all she'd had to dress this morning and to put make-up on. She'd not trusted herself to drive and, given she didn't remember the taxi ride here, that was a good decision. Better than some of the others, which had been haunting her this past week. Since before the funerals, the two coffins, side by side. She willed the image out of her head, concentrating on something else, anything else. She picked up a magazine from the table next to her and pretended to flip through it.

I should have been at the party. I never even

said goodbye. If I'd known that was the last time, I would have done better—been a better sister, a more attentive aunt. I thought there was more time. Stupid, stupid, stupid.

'Did the solicitor say what this was about?'

Giving up the pretence of magazine skimming, she turned to look at her companion. He'd already been waiting outside when she'd pulled up. The waiting room of the law firm was roomy, but he'd still taken the seat next to hers. Which was why his deep brown eyes were so close, leaving her feeling exposed under his scrutiny.

She'd caught him watching her a few times since…that day…a look of concern and wariness in his big dopey eyes. Those eyes almost seemed to see right through her, as if he could see the core of her, when no one else did. It had irked her immensely. Now, after this, it was torture. She wanted to tell him to leave, to go back to work and deal with his own grief. The one person in the world she had that knew both Ronnie and Harriet had to be him.

Ronnie and Harriet.

Her heart stopped working for a second. She felt the stutter in her chest when she thought of them. Of her sister, bloodied and broken on that gurney. RTA: three little letters that had taken their brother and sister away. They'd been going on a date and had ended up dead. The only saving grace was the fact that Zoe hadn't been with them in the car. She hadn't been lost too. She hadn't seen any of the horror of the aftermath, unlike Jackson and her.

Now they were both here, sitting in this waiting room, once again linked by family…only this time that family was gone for ever.

'Lucy,' he pressed. 'You with me?'

She had to look at the floor to get the answer out.

'He has the will. He said he needed to get things rolling. Are your parents not coming?'

Jackson shook his head. 'No. I spoke to Mum this morning. She didn't know about the meeting.'

'That's weird, isn't it?'

He shrugged. 'This whole thing's weird.'

'Was Zoe okay?'

His face brightened at the mention of their niece. 'Yeah, she's good. Mum said she's been a bit fussy but she's good.' His expression sobered. 'To be honest I think her being there is helping them hold it together.'

Lucy managed a nod. Anything else was blocked by the lump in her throat.

Jackson went to stand by the window, and she took him in for the first time. He looked dishevelled in the early afternoon light. She could make out minute wisps of grey in his longer than usual stubble and dark circles under his ever-seeing eyes.

'What? I know you want to say something.' He

didn't move an inch, aside from moving his lips. 'Out with it, Trigger.'

'Lucy,' she corrected automatically, irritated that he'd caught her studying him. 'You always say things like that. You don't know me, Jackson. You think you do because we were forced to spend so much time together. The only good thing to come out of this will be getting rid of you, actually. We won't have to pretend to get on any longer.'

'Nice. "Forced" was right. You are the prickliest pear I have ever met.'

'Prickly pear? What are you, five?'

'Yep, that's right.' His tone changed. 'I'll be six soon. Gonna buy me a cake?'

'You can shove your cake up your— What the hell are you doing?'

He strode across the room and knelt at her feet in one angry motion. When she went to get up from her seat, he stopped her.

'No, Lucy. What are you doing? Do you see anyone else helping you? We're waiting to see Harriet and Ronnie's solicitor. Harriet and Ronnie are dead!' The flicker of pain across his taut features was hard to miss. 'I know you've decided to just power through this in your usual way, but I'm a human! My little brother died. Your little sister died, and their little girl is here in this world all alone. Why do you not get that? Do you really not see anyone else? The whole hospital is devastated. We lost one of our own. My team is crying in the locker room between patients. Do you not see that?'

His eyes were wide, even darker than normal. 'Do you really not see me? I stood by your side at the funeral. Did you even realise I was there, Luce?' He sprang up, pacing to the window and back. 'I can't take this!'

There you go, you did it again—pushed too hard. He's right, who else have you got? You've chased everyone away. He has his parents. You have no one.

She took a steadying breath, willing her heart to stop racing. Her cheeks were flushed with shame and embarrassment.

'I'm sorry. I forget you lost someone too. I do care. I care about the people at work, about Zoe. I care that Harriet and Ronnie are…gone. I just deal with things my way. Grief is different for everyone.'

His sigh rattled the windowpane. 'Your way is to bottle it up. It's not healthy.' Lucy's eye-roll produced an irritated growl. 'See? There you go again, being all snarky when I am trying to get through to you.'

'I didn't say a word!'

'You don't have to! Your poker face doesn't work on everyone. It doesn't work on me. I just want to help, to make sure you face this properly.'

'I don't need your help, Jackson. I never did.' She jabbed a finger at her chest.

'Fine,' he snapped back, sitting at the farthest corner of the room. 'But this is not over, Luce.'

'Don't call me Luce,' was all she could spit back. No one called her Luce. It was Lucy or Dr Bakewell. Trigger was bad enough; he knew it wound her up. 'I don't need help. I'm fine. I just want to get this over with. Get back to normal. Get back to work.' The fact her manager had insisted on her taking a leave of absence didn't help. She needed to work. Rattling around her place, alone with her thoughts, was making her climb the walls.

'Right,' he scoffed. 'Whatever you say, Dr Bakewell.'

She busied herself with the contents of her handbag for a while, Jackson flicking through old magazines so hard she thought she heard some of the pages rip beneath his fingertips. After the longest twenty minutes in recorded history, a secretary came through a set of imposing double doors, inviting them in.

The solicitor's office was just as she remembered it from when her parents had died. A bookcase wall stuffed with weighty tomes provided the backdrop for Mr Cohen's huge walnut desk. The air smelled the same—a mixture of old books, paper and peppermint.

He greeted them at the door, his hair a little

greyer, his stature a little shorter, but still the same comforting presence.

'Miss Bakewell, you're all grown up!'

Lucy couldn't help but laugh. 'I am. How are you?'

She could feel Jackson at her shoulder, hear his awkward cough.

Mr Cohen didn't miss a beat. 'I'm well, thank you. This is Mr Denning, I presume?'

'Jackson, please,' he replied, the smile on his face as broad as it was genuine. Lucy had to look away. Behind that easy welcoming grin, she could see the taut expression as he exchanged pleasantries, see the hollows under his usually annoyingly sparkly eyes.

Stop it. You can't hold anyone else together. You are falling apart as it is.

'Please, take a seat,' Mr Cohen instructed.

Jackson took the chair next to hers, flexing his hands on the plaid leather arms.

'So,' Mr Cohen started, tiny little glasses perched at the end of his nose. 'As we discussed on the telephone, Harriet and Ronald left a will.' He eyed them both above the rims, pausing at the delicate nature of the conversation. 'It's pretty simple.' He eyed Jackson. 'Your parents were well aware of the contents of the will when it was written, and I have their agreement.'

Lucy sneaked a glance at Jackson, who looked as surprised as she felt. Harriet had never mentioned a will to *her.* Mr Cohen focused back on the papers in his grasp.

'Now, as to the financial aspects… It is instructed that the house be sold and any monies made as a result of said sale are to be put into a trust for Zoe.'

Lucy nodded along, barely listening as he spoke about jewellery and some other items of Ronnie's that were left to Jackson. The wedding rings were to be kept for Zoe. The pieces of Harriet's jewellery were to be shared between Lucy and Zoe. The ring from her mother was to go to Lucy, to be passed down to Zoe or any daughter Lucy had. Lucy sniffed at this, thinking of how Harriet had thought of her daughter and her, wanting things to be right and passed down to the future generations.

She willed her tears to stay away, blinking hard to clear her field of vision. A movement at her side caught her eye. Jackson was gripping the chair arms so tightly, she could practically hear his nails scratch against the leather. Her own hands flexed, and she held them together on her lap to stop herself from reaching out to him.

Stay strong.

Mr Cohen's professional tones pierced through her rampant thoughts a second later.

'As for the care of Zoe, Lucy Bakewell and Jackson Denning are named as her guardians, and are to raise said child together in a home to be determined by the beneficiaries. This will be subject to an initial six-month review to ascertain that this arrangement is working for all parties and benefits all parties. Any monies left in the deceaseds' accounts after all debts are paid are to be used for the purposes of raising said child, and the trust can be accessed through myself if further financial assistance is required.'

The money stuff didn't even enter Lucy's head. She was still baulking at the first part. Jackson looked like a clenched-jawed waxwork.

'I'm sorry,' she spluttered eventually when the sentence that had just rocked the very axis of her world had absorbed into her already addled brain. 'What was that? Joint custody? Me?' She jabbed a finger to her right. 'With him? Not Ronnie's parents—us?'

Joint custody? Is this a joke?

Zoe had been with the Dennings since the night of the crash. They were parents already. She'd just assumed… Well, she hadn't thought about it. Ronnie's parents had had Zoe that night, as they'd been babysitting. It had made sense for her to stay there until things were sorted. Until after the funerals were over and until Lucy was back at work. She'd just assumed that was what would happen and what they would want. She'd thought she and Jackson would just be there, Zoe's aunt and uncle, like always.

'Mr Cohen, I might be being dumb here, but I don't get it. There must be a mistake.'

Mr Cohen didn't look surprised at her reaction. In fact, he almost looked as if he found it rather comical.

'There's no mistake, Miss Bakewell. The instructions are clear. They were made when Zoe was born.'

Two years. Two years and no one had said a word.

Rounding on Jackson, she poked him hard in the arm. 'I'm supposed to raise Zoe? Me? With him?' He didn't even flinch. Her finger almost snapped as it hit a solid wall of tensed muscle.

'Yes, Miss Bakewell.'

'Lucy, please. This can't be right.' She looked at Jackson again. 'Did you know about this?'

He shook his head, leaning forward and putting it into his hands. 'No, of course not. Mum was being weird, but—'

'But what?'

'But she's just lost her son.' His tone was sober, flat.

'Right.' Lucy nodded. 'Right, okay. Sorry.'

Mr Cohen shuffled some papers in his file. 'I assure you, both Harriet and Ronald—'

'Ronnie,' Jackson corrected.

Mr Cohen pressed his lips tightly together. 'Of course. Harriet and Ronnie were very clear in their instructions. We discussed it at some length.'

'Yeah, well, they didn't tell me!' She was spewing her thoughts out loud now. 'I mean, I thought I might be named. It crossed my mind: I'm Harriet's only family. But why Jackson?'

'Why not?' Jackson pressed back. 'He was my brother. I know Zoe.' His eyes were darting all over the room. Lucy realised he was processing the news too. She was watching his freak-out in real time, as he was hers. She was wringing her hands, still waiting for him to erupt when he let out a surprised little chuckle. 'Ronnie, man.' He kept laughing. 'Well played, man.'

Lucy was apoplectic. 'This is funny to you? Are you freaking kidding me? Mr Cohen, why are the grandparents not named?'

Mr Cohen steepled his fingers together. 'Mr and Mrs Denning are well into their retirement. It was felt that the best chance of long-term stability for Zoe was for her to be raised by the pair of you.'

Lucy took it in, remembering times she'd dealt with patients in situations like this, with injured children orphaned by catastrophe. She'd dealt with enough social workers to see the logic. She and Jackson were both young, financially secure. They owned property. It made sense, if one didn't know their relationship. They bickered and taunted each other. HR had made them sign a waiver due to their legendary spats. They were so sick of hearing about complaints one made about the other they'd drafted a 'friendship agreement', as if Lucy and Jackson were toddlers fighting over the same toy at playgroup. Now they were supposed to sign up for a child together?

No. Not happening.

'Fine.' She sighed, finding her shields and barracking herself behind them. She would do what she did when her parents had died. She'd be the mother figure. She'd raise Zoe. She'd helped raise her little sister; she could do this, but she wasn't a team player. 'I am Harriet's only living relative. Zoe's aunt by blood. I don't need a co-parent in this.'

'Oh, really?' Jackson's voice was a gravelly hum. 'I didn't even know you were thinking about taking Zoe on.'

'Taking her on? She's not some project, Jack!'

'And you can't do this alone, Luce!'

Her fist slammed down on the desk before them and made a loud thump.

'Don't call me Luce! You know that drives me crazy!'

Mr Cohen made a loud, 'Ahem,' silencing them both.

'Sorry,' they both mumbled in unison. They were toe to toe, in each other's faces. Slowly, they sheepishly returned to their seats.

Mr Cohen's sigh ruffled the papers in front of him.

'I know that this has been awful. For both of

you. I did try to insist that the pair of you were informed beforehand, in case this event did occur, but Harriet was…reluctant.' His lips thinned. 'I suppose they never thought this day would come. I wish it hadn't myself, but the instructions were clear. Ronnie and Harriet wanted the best for little Zoe, and they chose you—together.

'Now…' He turned over the paper, pushing his glasses back up his nose. 'If one or both of you wish to object to this, or relinquish your guardianship, then there are contingencies in place.'

Zoe went to open her mouth to yell, *hell, yes*. She couldn't live and raise a child with her work nemesis, but Mr Cohen beat her to the chase.

'Lucy,' he addressed her. 'I have seen you and your sister navigate hard times before, and make no mistake, Harriet was the driving force behind this. Ronnie was on board, of course, but your sister, as you know, was a very determined planner. Even in death, she wanted the best. To that end, she left you this.' He opened the file and Lucy's eyes took in her sister's neat script across the surface of a crisp, cream envelope. 'I'll give you a moment. Jackson, would you like to follow me? We have refreshments waiting.'

Lucy didn't take her eyes from the envelope as the two men shuffled out of the room and didn't take in their muted voices or their back and forth. As soon as the door clicked closed, she reached and tore open the thick paper, her eyes brimming as she saw her sister's final words laid bare before her.

Dear Big Sis,

If you're reading this, then the worst has happened. I'm gone, and my Ronnie too. I'm sorry I had to leave you, dear Lucy, but I want you to know that I love you. Fiercely. Always have, despite our differences. When we lost our parents, you barely into adulthood yourself, it bonded us for ever, but divided us too. I might have been the little sister, but you were always much more than an annoying older sibling to me. When Mum and Dad died, you became my parent too. My role model.

When I fell apart, you were the one who told me to buck up. To get up and get on with it. To be strong, to face things head on. To never give up. To stop being stubborn.

So that's what I am asking...telling...you to do now. Buck up, big sister. Get up and get on with life. I mean this with the greatest affection, but you're not doing the best job of that now. I know you love your career, but somewhere along the way—between holding me together and sticking families back together—you lost a piece of yourself. That little girl who danced with me to the radio in our mother's kitchen knew that life was fun. I miss that girl, miss that part of you. I see it in Zoe already, in her tiny, joyful little face. I hope she keeps it.

I know we didn't always see things the same way, but I know you love us. Love Zoe. She's a beautiful baby and, writing this, I just know that you will be there to watch her grow. To give her strength and gumption. You taught her mother the same things.

I also realise that right about now, you're feeling pretty mad too. The control freak in you will be fuming with me. Don't be mad at Ronnie's parents. We asked them not to say anything. They deserve to enjoy their retirement. To be grandparents and not parents again. It's too much for them. This is the right thing and, one day, you'll see it too.

You're probably giving poor Jackson hell. You two are more alike than you think. I'm laughing from heaven right now at the rage I know you're feeling at me too. Our solicitor wigged out when I told him this was to be our little secret, but I knew, if I told you, you would have gone mad—not see the plan I have in my head. Be nice to Mr Cohen, he was always good to us. He steered us through our parents' deaths, and he'll see you all through mine too.

Back to Jackson. While you are my ride or

die, don't forget that Jackson just lost his too. Try not to torture him so much. Ronnie was worried not telling you both would make it harder, like some cruel final trick played on the two of you, but I have never been more sure of anything since meeting Ronnie that this is the right thing. I had you, and only you. I don't want that for Zoe, or you. Putting the burden of raising our child solely on your shoulders wouldn't be right. Jackson and you will need each other, like it or not.

Zoe will need people. She's already lost too much. I know you can guide our daughter to be fierce and brave. Braver and fiercer than I ever was. Jackson can tell her stories about her dad, help his memory stay alive for Zoe, like your memory of me will. He can be the dad that we had for that short time. The man she'll compare all those after against—someone to fix her bike, tell her to drive safely. Check the tyres on her car before she drives to college. And yes, you did that for me, but we missed Dad more than ever in those moments.

Jackson will be the one to protect her, to look after you both. You deserve someone to take care of you, even though I know you'll struggle to let him. Ronnie knows he won't leave, but try not to break him or send him away. I don't want you to struggle in this world alone, like we had to.

So, darling sister, my rock, my heart, my best friend—for once in your life, listen to your little sister and do what I wish. Don't shut people out, don't lose the softer parts of you. Be kind to Jackson and, if he wants to help, let him. You can shout at me later. I hope it's much later, dear sis. No more wishing life away, or letting it pass you by. Look after Zoe for us, and each other.

Ronnie and I love you all so much. I'll say hi to our parents for you. I'll see you when you get here.

Be brave, Lucy. I love you for ever.

Harry

Lucy jerked the letter away before her tears marred it. She read it twice more, the tears multiplying each time her eyes ran over the words.

'Oh, Harriet,' she said between shuddery breaths. She looked up to the ceiling, till the tears had dried on her cheeks. 'Way to play the sister card. You always, always knew how to pull a good guilt trip.' A sob escaped her. 'I can't even argue with you! Kind of hard to hash it out with you now.' She wiped at her face, wanting to pull herself back together. To get out of this room, this funk, and get back to doing.

I'm better moving forward. If I wallow in this, stay still, I'll be done.

She drew a deep, shuddery breath into her lungs. 'One more minute,' she said to her sister. 'One more minute, and then I'll get up.' Looking at the clock, she sobbed quietly as she watched the seconds on the clock tick down.

When she emerged from the room, the letter tucked into her bag, the two men were standing there. Jackson searched her face, as if he was looking for clues, and she scanned his.

Can I do this? Can we really live together? Can I raise a child, with a man who irritates the hell out of me?

All she could hear was her sister's voice in her head. The words from the letter were embedded in her brain for eternity. She thought back to when it had just been the two of them, parentless and alone, so much older, more aware, than poor Zoe. They had memories Zoe would never have, as painful sometimes as they were to recall.

The moment we knew we were alone.

She recalled vividly drying her sister's tears that day, telling her she would look after her, that everything was going to be okay. She knew just what to do then. She'd lived through this before. She could do it again and, as before, she would look after her niece. Her family. No matter what the personal cost.

'I don't want to contest the will,' she said, her voice a ghost of its usual self. 'Jackson?'

It suddenly occurred to her that *he* might want to. All this was new to him too. It didn't help that, for once, his usually very expressive face was like stone, immovable and impenetrable.

'Jackson what?' He also seemed to be playing dumb.

Was he playing for time?

She felt her heart thud in her chest.

Do I want him to say yes?

It was watching his stone-cold face that begged another question, one that she hadn't asked before.

What if he doesn't, and I am going to be alone in this anyway? I've hardly been nice to him.

She remembered what he'd said, about being by her side. He had been. He'd held her up at the funeral. He'd sorted out both their work leaves, though she'd chewed his ear off, even though he'd been right about them both needing the time off. He'd been there, every day, looking after Zoe, his parents and her. He'd rung her daily, offering to bring over food. She'd never said yes, but he'd tried.

As confused as he made her feel sometimes, he was always there—whether she wanted him to be or not. This was a big shock to both of them and, right now, he was so angry with her she couldn't tell which way the storm was blowing his sails.

His deep-brown eyes grabbed her the instant

she dared look him in the face. 'So, do you want to? Contest the will, I mean?'

She felt her face flush.

'No,' he said, his voice even, soft. 'I don't want to contest.' The bite of his lip gave his worry away. 'Unless you want me to.'

She thought back to her panic seconds earlier: the prospect of doing this on her own; the letter from her sister that felt like a burning hot poker in her bag. Whether she liked it or not, they were in this together. Zoe needed people who loved her, who understood her. A mother's last wish couldn't be ignored over her own barriers.

Six months. Give it six months.

'We'll have a lot to organise.'

A slight nod was all she got at first. The tension in the room was so palpable she could have cut it with a scalpel.

'We've got time,' he added with a sad little smile. 'We'll figure it out, right?'

CHAPTER FIVE

AFTER SIGNING AWAY what felt like their whole lives, an hour later the pair of them stumbled out into the daylight. When Lucy reached for her phone, Jackson put his hand over the screen.

'Don't get a taxi. I'll drive you.' Before she could tell him to move his hand, he cut her off. 'Get in the car, Lucy.'

They headed towards Jackson's car in silence, her head full of all the things they had to consider. Mr Cohen had explained that a date would be set for six months' time to confirm that the arrangement was working. If both parties agreed, and everyone was satisfied that Zoe was well cared for, the arrangement would continue. Six months to figure out how to co-parent with the Head of A&E, a man who was the subject of her tongue lashings and was now going to play 'Mummy and Daddy' with her.

'Whoa!' She felt Jackson's hand around her waist, yanking her back, just as the honk of a car in front startled her. 'What the hell are you doing?'

She'd walked out into the road. The driver

wound his window down and shouted an obscenity in their direction.

'Get lost!' Jackson countered, his fist banging on the roof of the car. He spun her round, holding the tops of her arms tight. 'You okay?'

'Yeah. No. Not at all.' His concerned features softened; his gaze was fixed on hers as if he was checking her for injuries. He wouldn't find them. They were on the inside, buried so deep, no surgeon would be able to cut them away from the healthy flesh. 'This is not normal, right?'

His laugh surprised her, jolted her out of her melancholy.

'No, Luce, this is far from normal.' He put her arm through his and guided her to the car park. 'Come on; let's get out of here before you try to stop the traffic again.'

Lucy stared out of the window when the car came to a stop. She'd barely registered the car ride and, staring at the neat house in front of her, she wondered how long they'd been driving.

'Come on.' Jackson nudged her, coming to open her car door before she got a chance to object.

'Where are we? Shouldn't we get back?' Over the last ten days, the pair of them had spent most of their time at his parents' house or dealing with the funeral arrangements.

'Zoe's fine. I want to show you something.'

She shrank back into the passenger seat.

'You have to get out of the car for me to do that.' He held out his hand and she gave in.

'Fine.' She huffed, getting out on her own and following him up the neat stone path. 'Whose house is this?'

He answered her with a key, which fit neatly into the front door.

'My house. I realised you've never actually been here.' He bent to pick up the post, stopping when he saw she was frozen on the doorstep. 'You can cross the threshold, you know. I disabled the booby traps and removed the garlic cloves, Elvira.'

She stepped over the threshold into a large, well-decorated hallway. He put the pile of post down on an end table near the door, rolling his eyes and pulling her in far enough to shut the door behind them both.

'And why are we here?'

His head snapped back at the question. 'Well, Zoe can't stay with my parents for ever. Now we know what's going on, we need to start making some decisions. Since you live in a one-bedroom flat, I thought we'd make this place our base.'

Our base. Our...base...

'What makes you think I'd want to live here?'

'The one bedroomed flat was the first clue. I have three bedrooms, a garden, space for all your and Zoe's stuff. It's not too far from work and... you're bugging out.'

Lucy closed the jaw she didn't know had been

gaping open, wrapping her arms tightly around herself as if she could shield herself from the lair of Jackson Denning.

'I'm not bugging out.'

'Did you tell your face that? You look like you're about to be sent to war.'

'Well…'

He headed down the hallway, pushing open a door at the end. She followed him into the kitchen which looked like a stainless-steel fortress. Jackson stuck his head in the fridge, pulling out various items, then moving over and lighting the stove.

'I thought we should eat, then I can show you around the place. The smallest bedroom is currently my office, but I can move things around. I can set up in the corner of the dining room or something.'

He cracked some eggs into a bowl, motioning for her to sit down at one of the stools set under the island. She looked around, trying to reconcile the man she knew with the one standing in front of her. 'Omelette okay?'

Her stomach grumbled. Sheila Denning was always trying to feed her, but she couldn't remember the last time she'd actually eaten anything substantial. 'Sure. Thanks.'

He shrugged his shoulders, getting to work cutting ham into little slices and grating cheese. She watched him work. For once, the silence wasn't entirely uncomfortable. The knives that usually cut through the air between them seemed to be resting in the drawer.

'I don't know why I've never been here before.'

He chuckled, mixing the ingredients in a large glass bowl.

'I know. I did invite you to the house warming, and a few barbecues, but you always said you were washing your hair.' He flashed her a sarcastic grin. 'You seem to wash your hair a lot. Remember when Arron from the fracture clinic kept asking you out? I'm pretty sure you gave him that same excuse for two months before he gave up.'

How did he know that? She thought she'd been discreet in turning him down.

'I remember,' she muttered, still distracted by the sight of Jackson doing something domestic. She was used to seeing him on the A&E floor, in scrubs or covered in blood. Today he looked different with his sleeves rolled up, his corded forearms flexing as he spooned the mixture into a frying pan. 'So, you own this? It's pretty big.'

'I bought it as a long-term investment.' He shrugged. 'I thought I might have a family one day, you know? I hate flats. I spent too much time in temporary digs whilst working away to live like that again—no gardens, thin walls. A buddy of mine's a builder, and he updated it for me. I like having the space. When I had a flat, I felt like I was on top of people, you know? Being so busy at work all day, the chaos, the noise; it batters the senses after a while.'

He pushed a plate holding a folded-up omelette over to her, together with cutlery. 'It's quiet here. I sit in the garden sometimes and have a beer, or fire up the grill. It's nice.'

He spoke about living here as if it was a foregone conclusion, and that got her hackles up.

'So you want us to live here just like that?'

He took a seat next to her with his own food, tucking in. 'It makes sense. It's near to work, there's room for two cars. You can have your own room. Space for us all.'

He noticed she wasn't eating, gently nudging her arm with his. Cutting off a piece, she popped it into her mouth. 'Wow.' It was quite possibly the best omelette she'd ever had, fluffy and filling. 'This is good.'

His bashful grin told her he didn't do this a lot. 'I like to cook too.' He waved his fork around the kitchen. 'State of the art.'

'Bragger. Bet you tell that to all the conquests you bring here too.'

He almost choked on his omelette. 'Conquests?'

'Yeah; Ronnie told Harriet things.' His brows shot up into his hairline. 'Sisters talk too.'

'Nice!' He huffed. 'Cheers for that, brother.' He saluted the ceiling, and they both went quiet, reminded of their loss.

'That's a point, though—dating.'

She felt him stiffen at her side.

'I didn't realise you were seeing someone.'

'I'm not.' She laughed at the absurdity, snorting by accident.

'All right, Miss Piggy.'

'Shut up!' She jabbed him with an elbow. 'I didn't mean to!'

His shoulders were shaking with mirth. 'Oh, I know, but that was funny. I intend to make you snort more often.'

'Jerk,' she said, but she was laughing along with him.

'You're really not dating, at all?'

She shook her head, finishing off the last morsels of food on her plate. 'Nope. No time for all that.' She thought of Zoe. 'Guess that won't be changing any time soon either, but if you date anyone we'll have to come up with some kind of plan.'

Jackson stood, collecting their empty plates and stacking them neatly into the dishwasher.

'I won't,' he said simply, leaning back against one of the tall, shiny, steel cupboards. 'I didn't do it much anyway, and never here.'

Wait, what?

'Never?'

'Nope.' He chuckled as he came over and pulled her to her feet. 'You'll be the first woman to sleep over, believe it or not.' He yanked her up so fast that she wobbled on her feet. Steadying herself against his chest with her hands, she looked up at him and heard his surprised gasp before she stepped back a little. He licked his lips and withdrew. 'Er… I'll show you around, then we'd better get back.'

He strode away, and she saw his fists clench together at his sides.

That was... They'd been...close.

'You coming?' he asked from the doorway.

'Yep.' She shrugged herself out of…whatever that had been. The last couple of weeks were giving her whiplash. She thought of her sister's letter, looking around at Jackson's house. Could she really live here, give up her life? Taking a deep, galvanising breath, she went to find Jackson.

'I think it's only fair if you see my place,' she said when she found him in the living room. 'Before we make any firm decisions.'

To his credit, he readily agreed. 'Fine; we have time. I've shown you mine,' he said with a wink. 'Let's see what you've got.'

'You can't be serious.'

There was no mistaking his mocking tone and, now she was here, she couldn't blame him. Compared to his place, her flat was a little on the small side. She'd never needed a big home, and had never wanted the expense or felt the need to rattle around in some huge, posh abode. She didn't have the time for decorating, and she didn't entertain. She was barely at home—she usually took extra shifts, ended up at the gym or went out with friends or with her sister. Her days off at home were usually spent sleeping or doing laundry so she didn't have to wear the grungy undies at the back of her drawer on the next shift at work. Having Jackson standing in her kitchen, rooting through her fridge, she almost felt silly at feeling so stubborn.

'Smells like something died in here.' He pulled out an old pizza box, opening it and retching.

Oh, yeah, I forgot about that tuna and sweetcorn pizza I had in there. When did I order that—last week?

He looked around the neat, little unused kitchen. 'Bin?'

She shrugged, taking the box from him. 'I usually just use plastic bags and take them out daily.'

He raised a brow but said nothing. 'I'm not here a lot. I don't really eat here.'

'Zoe will, though.' He motioned around him. 'This place is nice, but my place is a house, with a garden—like she's used to. I know that you want to keep your life, but maybe… Oh, I don't know.' He seemed to shrink into himself. Even then she had to look up to meet his eye line. 'It's only been a couple of hours. I can't tell you what to do; I don't know myself.'

'I don't know either, that's the problem. It's a lot to take in.' She joined him in peering at the fridge innards. 'Wow, it does stink.' Leaning forward, she pulled out a takeaway box that was pretty much mush. She couldn't even remember what it *had* been, let alone when she'd ordered it. 'Oh, my Lord, it smells like medical waste.'

'Told ya,' he muttered and, when she caught his eye, she couldn't help but laugh. He dissolved into laughter along with her, and the two of them were laughing hysterically in seconds. 'I knew you usually ate at work. Now I know why. It's not like the canteen food is that good.'

She wanted to bite back at him but couldn't stop laughing long enough to get any words out. She laughed till her sides hurt, Jackson laughing along with her. He leaned against the counter when their laughter subsided, looking around him at her home. He was here, in her space. The fact it wasn't the weirdest thing that had happened that day didn't make it any less…odd.

'I can't believe you're standing in my kitchen and we were laughing again. Us laughing in kitchens is becoming a habit.' She pulled her hair back into a bun and fastened it with a couple of chopsticks she pulled from her cutlery drawer—her very spartan cutlery drawer. 'It's been a weird day.'

'A weird time,' he said with a rueful smile. 'It's not a bad place. I hope you don't think I was—'

'I don't.' Lucy pulled a large disposable bag from a stack in the drawer, getting to work on emptying the fridge. 'I'm kind of a slob, I get it.'

She looked around at the barely used utensils in the pot on the side. 'Harriet bought that for me. She said it would encourage me to cook more.' Her voice cracked, and she fell silent. Yesterday she'd had a different life, now she was barrelling blindly into a new one. Still, there was no time to stop. Stopping meant dwelling.

She threw more things into the bag, not even caring what the food was now, whether it was in date or spoiled. It didn't matter any more. She'd known the second she'd walked back into her flat that she wouldn't be bringing Zoe back here Her home was for her old life. She dumped the bag on the floor and walked over to Jackson. 'You knew what you were doing, didn't you, bringing me here after your place?'

Jackson folded his arms, watching her as if he was waiting for her to say more before he reacted. He had a tendency to do that, she noticed. She noticed more things about him these days. Probably because she couldn't exactly walk away from him, or pretend he was on the outskirts of her life any more, a bug to be swatted. She felt his hurt as keenly as her own.

'I'm not judging how you live, Lucy. I know how hard you work. Harriet told me you always looked after her. Living alone, it's different. Working long hours, those things are not as important.'

'I know, but you're right. Your house…well… it's a house, for a start. Zoe is used to having a garden to play in. She has that swing set at her house. I can't exactly hang it off the balcony, can I? I don't have a bedroom for her. I have one allocated car parking space; you have a driveway.' She picked up the bag of spoiled food, reaching for her handbag. 'Let's go see Zoe, okay? We have the six-month review to prepare for.' She lifted the food bag and waggled it at him. 'I think we might need to get a plan together.' As she walked to the door, his voice stilled her.

'Grab some clothes too.'

Her head snapped to look at him. 'Why?'

'I have a bottle of Scotch I've been saving.' His lips curled into a smile. 'I think our life-merging plans might need a two-drink minimum.'

She didn't argue with him on that one. Leaving the food bag by the front door, she headed to the bedroom to grab her overnight bag.

The sun was barely up in the sky when Lucy looked out of the large, decaled window. She'd sneaked out early from Jackson's, intending to go to her place and pick up some more of her stuff. After seeing Zoe and Sheila and Walt, Jackson's parents, they'd been too drained to talk much. His parents had been so apologetic about keeping the contents of the will a secret from them. The relief on both their faces was obvious, and Lucy hated that they'd had to shoulder that on top of burying their son and daughter-in-law.

When they'd got back to Jackson's house after putting Zoe to bed at his parents' house, the events of the day had felt enough. Instead of making plans, they'd opened the Scotch, put on some dumb action movie and ordered a takeaway. They'd talked about work, their patients; they'd swapped stories each had never heard before.

She'd headed to bed early, feeling awkward going up to the spare room. She'd spent half the night staring at the ceiling. In the end she'd tiptoed back downstairs, taking another full tumbler of the good stuff to bed to try and knock herself out for a few hours.

Instead of heading home, she got the cab to stop at the coffee shop near work. She needed something familiar, something that hadn't changed. Before work, she often met her colleague Amy for coffee. When she pushed through the steamed-up glass doors, seeing her friend there gave her a jolt of sorely needed comfort and she spilled her story.

'So that's it, you're a parent now?'

Amy, who worked with Lucy in Paediatrics, pushed her coffee closer to her. Lucy didn't reply for a moment, focusing on the pretty little leaf art on the surface. Picking up her spoon, she stirred the liquid, erasing the image, turning pretty perfection to swirling chaos.

'Not a parent, still an auntie. Just more…hands on.'

'Mmm-hmm.' When she finally met Amy's

eye, she could tell she wasn't buying it. 'That simple, eh? Any other person would be curled in a ball somewhere. I know you're tough, Lucy, but still; you must have so much to think about. It's been, what, two weeks? And Jackson—Daddy Denning? Mate, that's a lot.'

Lucy bit at her lip, buying time with a slow sip of her coffee. 'I know. I haven't even told work. The hospital gave us both time off, and we have to adjust to this new normal, I guess. Curling into a ball isn't going to get things sorted. Harriet left instructions for everything, but I still don't really know where to start.'

'And you have six months to get sorted before you make a final decision?' Amy was always a good listener, one of the few people Lucy trusted, other than Harriet. Seeing her confusion and shock brought home just how gargantuan her situation was. Perhaps she was still numb. Maybe curling into a sodden mess would come later. It hadn't with her parents' passing; she'd had to get on with things.

She ran her hands down her cheeks, realising that this time wouldn't be any different. She was glad that her autopilot button hadn't let her down again. She hadn't cried since being at the hospital. 'Seems like a short space of time for the rest of your life.'

'Yeah, but it's not like I'm going to walk away from Zoe.'

Amy sat listening with that look she always had: attentive, helpful. Ever since they'd started working together throughout early mornings, late nights and coffee shop breakfasts, Amy had been a good sounding board. Whenever they got to talking, she always got that look on her face, as if she was digesting everything and judging nothing. Lucy made a mental note to tell her one day how grateful she was for her friendship. She never really had, and the reminder that life was short had made her more aware of the few relationships she had and how important they were.

'I never said you would. Still, it's not like it's just for the six months. A kid takes eighteen years—minimum. My little brother Ben is twenty and still bringing his washing home from university for my mum to sort out. I swear, how that boy still doesn't know how to use a washing machine…'

Lucy laughed under her breath. 'I think it will be a while before we have to think about that.'

'Exactly!' Amy seized on her point. 'She's what, two? It's a long time to share your life with someone you don't even like, and what if you meet someone, or Jackson does?'

A couple of customers walked in, stopping their conversation. Lucy's phone buzzed in her pocket. Thinking it was work, she fished it out: *Jackson.* She'd left a note letting him know she'd gone out. It had felt weird, skulking out of a man's house. It was not something she usually did, not that any of this was usual.

Got your note. Everything okay?

It was weird to see him asking her that on a text. Normally they texted about work, the odd time about Harriet or Ron, but mostly they sent each other sarcastic memes or snippy comments. He was listed in her phone as 'Satan', for goodness' sake. She tried to remember her sister's letter, but still, the day to day was hard. How the hell were they going to navigate the next six months, let alone life beyond that?

Yeah. Is Zoe okay?

She's fine. My folks would have called us. Not why I was texting.

She texted back.

I went for a walk.

He knew Amy. Why hadn't she told him the truth? She'd slept over, not done the walk of shame! Looking around her, she envied the other customers, enjoying their morning pastries and coffees without the side of drama.

'Everything okay?' Amy asked, tapping her nails on the table top. 'You look guilty.'

Amy struck again, knowing how to read Lucy's usual poker face in an instant. She remembered Jackson's comment about how he could read her. Perhaps she trusted him more than she thought. She must do, for him to see through her defences.

'Jackson.' She waved the phone at Amy. 'He messaged me to see where I was.'

Amy's tattooed brows knitted together with the force of her frown.

'You didn't tell him? I thought you stayed over?'

Lucy's defences sprang up, along with her shoulder blades.

'I left a note!'

'Saying what?'

'Gone out?' Hearing it out loud made her wince. 'It's barely past seven; I didn't think he'd be up yet. I did nothing wrong.'

Amy checked her watch and began gathering her things. 'You did nothing wrong, but you can't just leave a note and go out early in the morning. You might have worried him, going off like that. You're going to be living together.'

Lucy opened her mouth to object, but Amy shut her down with a pointed finger. 'Before you say you have your own place, you're an independent woman, blah-blah-blah, the man opened his home to you. You live on salads, smoothies, caffeine and three hours' sleep. I've seen how you live and work, Lucy: laser-focused. You are more than capable of looking after yourself, but it's not about just you any more! Imagine if you were Jackson, just for a minute. You've hardly been yourself lately. Who would be?'

Amy got up to leave, pulling Lucy onto her feet for a hug. 'Take back some drinks and pastries with you and sort it out.' She winked. 'Go home, Lucy. For once, let someone in. Having someone to take care of you might not be so bad. That person being Jackson? It could be a lot worse.'

'I'm not sure about that,' Lucy whined. 'Take me to work with you instead!'

Amy laughed. 'No chance, Bakewell. Now, be the tough nut I know you are and face him. I think you might find things will work out better than you think.'

'You think?'

Amy grinned. 'I'd bet money on it.'

Jackson's front door was unlocked when she got back. It felt weird, just walking in without knocking, but she was laden down with the bribes Amy had suggested so she pushed through her nerves. He met her at the door, taking the coffee cups from her full hands.

'Thanks,' she muttered. 'I brought us some goodies. I thought I was going to drop the lot.' He walked off into the kitchen and she followed him sheepishly.

'You didn't need to go out for coffee.' He looked as if he'd just woken up, his usually perfect hair looking messed up. He was wearing a pair of grey tracksuit bottoms, his T-shirt one of some old band from their youth she'd never liked. She'd never had time for music growing up, other than to shut out her university cohorts in the library when she was studying. Even then it had been more emo-grunge-type stuff, rather than the hard rock Ronnie and Jackson had preferred to blast out. 'I have a pretty good coffee maker here.'

'I prefer the coffee shop.'

'Okay.' She put the box on the counter, and he opened it. 'Wow. I can see why.' He pulled an almond croissant out of the box and sank his teeth into it. 'Dear Lord of medicine, that's good.' He finished the whole thing in three bites.

'The coffee's decent too. I've been going there for years.' She side-eyed him. 'I'm sorry I slipped out.'

His cup was halfway to his lips but he paused. 'You don't have to answer to me; I'm not your parole officer. You left a note.'

'So why did you text me, then?'

'Because of the note.' He nodded to the fridge where her words sat, glaring at her like a beacon.

Gone out. Lucy

'Not exactly *War and Peace*, is it? I just wondered if you were okay, if you were somewhere safe.'

Lucy took a donut and ripped it in half. 'What did you want, GPS coordinates?'

'No, but we just lost… It would have been nice if you'd said where you'd gone, that's all.'

'Would you have done the same?'

He didn't hesitate. 'I will, yes. I know yesterday was a lot, but I do think that before we do this and go back to work we should make a few ground rules together, don't you? I know Zoe has a nursery to go to, but we should talk about when we are both on the same shifts, nights off…'

Thinking about the nursery reminded her of Harriet and a memory of when she'd first started there. On a rare day off, Lucy had been at the dry cleaner's in town when Harriet had called her, distraught. She'd managed to sob out a plea to meet her for coffee and Lucy had abandoned her pressed clothes on the counter and run the whole way.

'Thanks for coming.' Harriet had sniffed when Lucy got to her table, panting. 'I ordered for you.' She'd pointed to a large coffee, but Lucy didn't register it.

'What's wrong?' She'd been alone. 'Where's Zoe?'

'She's gone,' Harriet had croaked out.

'What?' Lucy had been about to have a full-blown panic attack when her sister had spoken again. 'She didn't even look back this morning. The nursery staff just took her and she went off, happy as a clam.'

Lucy sagged into her seat. 'Harriet, I thought something was wrong!'

'Something is wrong!' Harriet sniffed again. 'I wanted Zoe to go to nursery a couple of days a week to let her play with other kids, you know? I don't want her to feel different when she starts school, but…'

'She still very much needs you. You're her mother. Just because she goes to nursery doesn't mean that she's gone.'

'I know.' Harriet had glugged at her green tea. 'I just…didn't expect it to feel like that.' She'd wiped at her eyes, flashing a smile that told Lucy that she'd pulled herself together. Harriet had known how to do that. Lucy had always been a little jealous of that ability. Lucy did the opposite: she just pushed everything down. 'They grow so fast.'

'I know.' Lucy had taken her sister's hand in hers. 'You did the right thing. Zoe will make friends, learn new things. It's only two days a week. You have Zoe for the rest of your life. Years of holding her little hand.'

Harriet's returning smile had been dazzling that day.

'Thanks, sis, you always know the right thing to say to calm me down.'

'That's my job.'

Lucy remembered the warm feeling she'd felt from those words…

The memory faded, and she realised Jackson was looking at her expectantly.

'Yeah, we can do that—make a schedule. I really want to keep her at that nursery. Harriet would want that.'

'Then we keep it going,' Jackson agreed. 'I agree. Mum and Dad will help too. We can do it. Other people do, don't they?'

They were looking at each other just a little bit too intently when the silence was broken. Jackson's phone rang: *Mum* flashed up on the caller ID.

'I'll just grab a shower and let you get that.' She jumped off the stool and half-ran up the stairs, anything to avoid the domestic scene she'd just left.

'To be continued, Lucy!' he called up the stairs. She was pretty sure he heard her groan of anguish. *She* was pretty sure she heard him chuckling.

'This is going to be a nightmare,' she muttered under her breath.

CHAPTER SIX

WHEN LUCY CAME down from her shower, Jackson was ready and waiting with an invitation from his mother for dinner.

'Sure, that sounds nice, actually. Has she said anything about us taking Zoe?'

Jackson shook his head. 'She just said she'd give us time. You know, to sort things out here. I don't know what you were thinking, but I get the feeling my folks are pretty tired. They've had her since—'

'Yeah.' Lucy shuffled her feet. 'I know. They need time to grieve too, to rest.'

'Yeah,' Jackson echoed. The silence hung around them at the bottom of the stairs. 'We need to get on with it, I guess.'

Heaving out a sigh, Lucy rolled up the sleeves of her long T-shirt. 'Right—so we bring her here tonight after dinner.'

Jackson's brows raised, but he said nothing to contradict her. 'Okay, I have some boxes in the garage. We'd better get the office cleaned out. I read somewhere that kids need to be settled in their own room, so…'

'Yeah,' Lucy agreed. 'It's best if she has her

own room from the start. Gets a routine.' She narrowed her eyes. 'You read that where, exactly?'

The blush on his face was unmissable. 'Er…a parenting blog.'

She didn't want to laugh at that moment—it wasn't a happy moment—but she couldn't stop the smirk on her face from erupting. 'Right.' An odd kind of burble sprang up from her chest. 'Read many of those lately?'

'Laughing.' He smirked. 'Nice.'

She'd reached out to pat his arm before she realised. 'No, no. It's cute.' She laughed again, not bothering to supress it. 'Are you planning to breastfeed too?'

He grabbed her arm as she pulled back, as if he missed the contact. 'Ha! Funny!'

'I think so.' She cackled. They both noticed how close they were at the same time, and their arms dropped to their sides. 'So, you want to get the boxes?'

He cleared his throat. 'Er…yeah. I'll…er…see you up there.'

She heard the garage door open just as she was pushing open the wooden office door.

'Wow.' She breathed, and it wasn't seeing his office that took her aback. She knew that they'd been in the same space, but the contact, his hand on her bare skin, was still something alien.

Weird: that was the word for all of this.

Keep moving. Suck it up.

The office was pure Jackson. His desk was super-neat, like the rest of the house. Running her hand along the wooden surface, she picked things up, taking it in: little pots of rubber bands, paperclips and staples. The files on the shelves were all colour-co-ordinated, the same as his files at the hospital. His writing was a perfect set of uniformed letters, bold and confident, unlike her scribbly scrawl. *Everything in its place*, she mused. *So organised.* On the back wall above the desk, the pin board was full of photos, all neatly placed. There were photos of work nights out, a picture of Zoe wearing her Elsa dress, back when she'd been obsessed about being a cute little ice queen. Lucy laughed when she saw it, tears brimming in her eyes.

'I remember that outfit,' Jackson said from the doorway. She hadn't even heard him come up the stairs. Putting the flat-packed boxes to one side, he came to stand beside her. 'Harriet had to prise that dress off her every night for weeks.'

Lucy smiled. 'Yeah?' Jackson's aftershave was nice. It matched the room, she thought—light, but woodsy, strong but gentle somehow. 'She definitely knows her own mind.'

His head dipped closer as he took the board off the wall. 'I'll put this in my room for now.'

She reached for it, seeing something. 'Is that… us?' Jackson's gaze followed her finger to the photo in the centre. 'From the paintballing day?'

It was a group photo, a crowd of blues and reds, paint- and mud-splattered.

'I don't know.' He went to leave but she stopped him.

'It is!' She took the board from his grasp, leaning in to peer at the sea of faces. Jackson was laughing, head tilted to another player. When she found her own face in the crowd, she knew why—there she was, bright-red cheeks and mud smeared face, flipping him off. 'How do you even have this? That's so funny.'

When she turned to look at him, he looked as if he wanted the ground to swallow him up. 'Jackson?'

'I asked for it.' He shrugged, but the action was too forced to be real. 'No biggie.'

She passed it back, watching as he left the room.

What was that? He kept a photo of her where he could see it all the time?

She was still looking at the door when he came back, busying himself with making up boxes. He didn't meet her eye as he started to pack away the coloured files. Taking a box, she got to work, not sure what, if anything, she'd done wrong.

'It's a nice photo,' she muttered when she couldn't stand the awkward pause in their conversation any longer. He side-eyed her, and she witnessed the sag in his tight shoulders.

'I like it.'

* * *

It didn't take long to clear everything away. Putting the boxes in a neat stack in the corner, they got to work on the furniture.

'Careful,' Jackson warned as they navigated the stairs. 'Don't drop this desk and flatten me.' She pretended to consider it, a playful look on her face that made him shake his head.

'And raise a kid on my own? Death by desk would be the easier option.'

She felt his deep laugh through the desk, and the tension slid away. They managed not to maim each other getting the rest of the furniture down, which surprised them both.

They had just brought the last of the boxes down to the corner of the dining room that was now an office nook when she noticed the time.

'We need to go. We're going to be late for your mother.'

Looking around the now empty third bedroom, Jackson sighed. 'I forgot about dinner. Least we got this done. The blinds will do for now, till we can decorate at least. What does she have in her room again?'

Lucy tried to remember what Zoe's room looked like. It felt as if she'd not been there for ever.

'I think it was still decorated as a nursery. Yellow, maybe?' She rubbed her forehead. 'I know she has a cot bed, a dresser and a toy chest.'

Jackson was looking around the room as if he could picture it all in place.

'Cool. It should all fit, I think.'

The longer they were in there, staring at the furniture marks in the carpet, the closer the air felt. Lucy pulled at her T-shirt, feeling as if the collar was tightening around her neck somehow.

'Is it hot in here? I feel hot.' She went to the window, opening it and gulping at the air. 'I can't get my breath.'

'Lucy? Are you okay?'

Her chest was so tight, she felt she couldn't breathe. 'I… No… I…'

She felt Jackson's arms around her. 'It's okay. You're okay.'

'How is this okay?' she managed to push out. 'This was your office, and now it's a kid's room! How are you just okay with this?'

'Breathe,' he kept saying over and over in an even voice. 'It's okay. We'll be okay.'

When the panic released her long enough to cry, she bawled, gut-wrenching, stomach-hurting sobs. 'It's not my house. It's not Zoe's house. It shouldn't be like this, and we're just playing house and pretending that the world's not on fire.'

'I know,' he mumbled, his arms holding her tight, which for once she didn't even think to object to. They were necessary to hold her up, hold her together. 'We can do this. I promise, Luce. Rent your place out, move in here and we'll bring Zoe home. Do this one day at a time, okay? Breathe. You're okay.'

Listening to his voice, she looked around the bare room.

'I'm rubbish at painting,' she muttered when her breathing was even. She felt his laughter jolt her as they stood squished together. 'Don't laugh.'

His hand rubbed circles along her back. She felt her skin warm from his heat, her muscles unclench.

'I'll get you a paint gun.' His deep voice was full of warmth too. 'I seem to remember you could handle that.' She huffed, squeezing him to her like a reflex, before stepping away. This touching thing was getting out of hand.

Wiping her tears, she widened the gap between them. 'Come on; your mother will be worried if we're late.'

She didn't see the expression on Jackson's face when she left the room but the deep, throaty 'I'll drive' sent an oddly familiar shiver down her spine.

Keep it together, she told herself for most of the car ride over. *Grief does strange things to us all.*

Sheila and Walt were happy to see them both, but the fatigue on their faces was evident. When Jackson said they'd like to take Zoe home, they didn't object. They had dinner, and before they knew it, the pair of them were driving away with Zoe in the back seat, a load of toddler paraphernalia and enough food in containers to feed them for a week.

A couple of hours later, Zoe was well and truly making her presence known. Sheila and Walt had packed a travel cot and some supplies for them but they'd barely had a chance to set it all up before Zoe started to scream the place down.

'I wonder if she's just unsettled,' Jackson tried to say over the noise of her ear-splitting screams. 'I read that kids pick up on things, even when really young. Emotions, changes, you know.'

'You think?' Lucy snapped back, panic overruling every sane thought in her body. 'I'm not stupid, Sasquatch. My medical speciality trumps your parenting blogs.'

'Never said you were stupid, Trigger.' His jaw tensed, making his whole cheek judder from the sudden tightening. 'I hate my nickname too, shorty!'

Zoe started to cry louder the second he raised his voice, and both of them stilled. She could see the tension in Jackson's jaw as he lifted her higher up in his arms. 'Hey, Zo-Zo, it's okay! You hungry?'

'We tried that.' She pointed to the spaghetti hoop stain on her hoodie. 'We've tried changing her, she won't go to sleep...' The wailing intensified the second Jackson tried to put her down on the floor.

'She had a nap earlier but Mum said it was barely twenty minutes.'

Jackson lifted Zoe onto the kitchen counter. 'Does she feel warm to you? She's not warm, is she?'

Lucy placed a cool palm on the little girl's forehead. 'A little. No fever, though, I already checked her temperature earlier and it's normal.'

Zoe was sobbing now, tears spilling down her cheeks as her whole face went beetroot-red.

'Is she thirsty? What about a drink?'

'She'd a beaker of milk at dinner, and she had—what?—sips of juice half an hour ago.'

'What?' Zoe's wails had drowned out her words.

'Sips of juice!' she repeated, retrieving the beaker of cold apple juice from the fridge and showing him the measuring scale. 'See? It was at the top before.'

Jackson frowned. 'Maybe we should take her into work.'

'For crying? I'm not going into work for that. We'd get laughed out of the place!' Lucy scoffed, picking a now screaming Zoe up and passing her the beaker. Zoe screeched harder and knocked the cup away. 'Have a drink, come on.' She tried again, and this time Zoe pelted the beaker across the kitchen. The ear-splitting decibels she emitted make them both jump. 'We don't need to take her in.'

'Well, I don't know what's wrong. It could be a stomach-ache.'

Lucy didn't answer. She was too busy running irrational scenarios in her head. Her training was lost to her as she ran through every possible condition from hand, foot and mouth to meningitis…and the screaming thought that Zoe knew she had been left to her aunt and uncle and was just distraught at their lack of parenting skills. Trying to stop her inner panicked monologue from giving her another panic attack with her niece in her arms, she took her through to the lounge and tried to lay her down on the sofa. Zoe's whole body went as rigid as an ironing board so she gave in and changed tack.

You can do this, she told herself. *You save babies on a daily basis. Heck, figure it out!*

'Will you just hold her a second? I'll check her tummy, but I don't think it's to do with her digestion.'

She tried to lift Zoe up to pass her off to Jackson, but she was screaming blue murder and rigid everywhere but her legs. Her legs were not stiff; they were quite the opposite, in fact. She was windmilling them, kicking both of them as she bellowed at the top of her lungs.

'Let me, just… Zo-Zo! You're okay, darling. Let Auntie Lucy have a look at you.'

Jackson finally managed to get a grip on her, holding her up and out as if she was a bomb and he was a rookie disposal expert. 'She's like an eel! Hurry up, Trig!'

Lucy was trying to lift up Zoe's little top, but it was like wrestling an anaconda in the midst of an air raid siren.

'Don't call me that! I'm trying; I don't want to hurt her!'

'Hurt her?' Jackson half-shouted over the ear-splitting wails. 'She's got more kick than a striker! I've treated easier drunks in A&E! Just pull her top up!'

'I'm trying!' She managed to do a quick examination, trying to remember her years of training and experience—and not get kicked in the face. 'Her stomach's normal, no blockage. She had a bowel movement earlier—that was normal too.'

Jackson went to put her down on the floor, but she lifted her legs away, clinging to his clothing.

'Well, what's left? Exorcism?'

'That's not funny,' she half-yelled back. 'And, for the record, you're a doctor too!'

'Yeah, well, I'm just waiting for her head to spin round.' He tried to soothe her in his embrace, his hand over one cheek. 'She's not hot, but her cheeks are.'

The pair of them looked at each other at the exact same time. 'Teething,' they said in unison.

Jackson pulled his car keys out of his pocket.

'The supermarket—they have a pharmacy that is open late.'

Lucy was already grabbing her bag.

'Good thinking.' She rubbed at her head where a bitter headache was beginning to form. 'I'll get her coat.'

* * *

The coat didn't get closer to Zoe than the back seat. She turned purple when Lucy came near her with it, and Jackson turned a ghostly shade of white and muttered something about her throwing up in his back seat. It took them ten minutes to get Zoe to bend enough to fasten her into the car seat, and by then they were both so frazzled they just wanted to get to the local supermarket without driving the car into the nearest brick wall.

Jackson backed out of the driveway at a slow crawl.

'Jackson, the supermarket closes in three hours. Any chance you could drive faster?'

He pulled onto the main road, Zoe's wails now receding into shuddering sobs with the movement of the car. She loved the motion, Lucy remembered. Harriet and Ronnie used to drive her round together when she wouldn't sleep.

He made a throaty huffing noise. 'Last time I was in a car with you driving, I got whiplash. We have a kid on board.'

'Yeah, well, a toddler on a trike would beat you in a race. She's not a new-born.'

'Yeah, thanks for that, Mrs Paediatrician.'

'That's Ms Paediatrician, actually, and you're welcome.'

A car pipped its horn behind them. When they both looked, they were greeted by a pensioner behind the wheel who promptly mouthed, 'Put your foot down!' at Jackson.

Turning to face the front, Zoe now quiet in the back, cheeks aflame, Lucy pressed her lips together.

'Don't say it,' Jackson droned, putting his foot down. Lucy laughed all the way to the supermarket car park.

Zoe was like a different child the second they sat her in the trolley seat. Her cheeks were still flushed postbox-red, but she was happily looking around her as they strode down the aisles.

They both stopped dead when they came to the baby section the pharmacist had directed them to—very quickly, they noted, which probably had something to do with the people in the queue and the ear-splitting wails Zoe had produced in Lucy's arms. They reached two long rows of shelves filled with toys, equipment, toiletries and pregnancy gear.

'All this stuff? Really?' Jackson was clinging to the shopping trolley with white knuckles. Lucy arched a brow and charged forward. In that moment she had never been more grateful that she'd gone into paediatric medicine and not the cardiology specialism she'd once considered. Affairs of the heart she didn't know, but this, she knew. From watching Harriet and the parents of the patients she cared for, she'd picked up a few things along the way. For some reason, the fact that Jackson wasn't the polished A&E doctor he normally was helped too.

'Yep. It's a multi-million-pound industry, Jackson. You been living under a rock?'

'Nope, but that doesn't sound so bad about now. Ronnie didn't talk much about this side of things.'

Lucy headed straight for the teething gel, picking up a couple of boxes and chucking them into the trolley. Zoe was starting to grizzle again, the distraction of the bright lights and people wearing off in favour of her irritable gums. Sanitising her hands, Lucy ripped open one of the boxes and squeezed some of the gel out onto a finger.

'Er, shoplift much?' he teased.

Lucy jabbed him with her elbow and started to rub some of the gel onto Zoe's gums. The little girl pulled a face at first, but then settled down. The relief was evident, and Lucy felt a small frisson of achievement.

'Well, that worked,' Jackson said, a touch of wonder in his words. He went over to the shelf and picked up another five boxes. 'We need to stock up on that. What else can we get? I'm guessing that they don't have holy water in their range.'

He was looking up and down the products, and Lucy couldn't help but smile as she pushed the trolley and watched him taking everything in. He was quite funny as an uncle. She'd always known that he loved Zoe, but seeing him take such an interest made her think that perhaps Harriet and Ronnie had not been so far off the mark. If she'd been alone with Zoe screaming the place down in her little unkempt flat, would she have been here now, so calm, getting supplies? She knew the answer to that—*heck no.* She'd either have driven to work in a panic to get help or been online, desperately looking for same-day-delivery miracle purchases to help her out.

'Hey.' Jackson shook her out of her thoughts, waggling a teething ring at her. 'These things go in the fridge; the cold is supposed to help soothe the gums. What do you think?'

Lucy pushed the trolley closer. 'I think we should get some.' She pulled a pack of pull-ups off another shelf. 'Let's get stocked up.'

Jackson's dark-brown eyes locked onto hers for a moment longer than she was used to.

'Deal.' The corner of his mouth turned into that smile she secretly liked, the one he'd flashed the day they'd met all that time ago. 'I say we get some alcohol too.' He grinned. 'For the adults—we deserve a treat too.'

'Double deal!' She laughed, pulling another pack of pull-ups off the shelf. 'Fifty-fifty, though, right? Anything we spend has to be fifty-fifty.'

She could swear his eyes sparkled. Supermarket lighting, she told herself, blinking hard.

'Fifty-fifty all the way.'

CHAPTER SEVEN

'ARE YOU SURE your parents didn't mind having her again? I feel like we're putting a lot on them. They've just had her for over two weeks solid.'

They were sitting in Jackson's car the next day, parked at the front of Harriet's and Ronnie's house. They were both exhausted after Zoe's first night in her new home. Her bedroom was a priority, now it was emptied. The travel cot looked sad in there all on its own. The poor little love had been unsettled, meaning that they'd each slept in fitful shifts. Over one of Sheila's lasagnes and a bottle of red, they'd also managed to sort out a rota system for who did what, and Lucy had ordered a wall calendar online for when they went back to work. They'd been so tired and distracted from Zoe that they hadn't even fought about any of it—progress.

'She can start back at nursery soon, help give them a break. Mum offered—she'll take Zoe to nursery when we're at work, and pick her up when we need her to. She has a key for my—*our*—place already. Trust me, they want to help. When I dropped Zoe off, Dad practically ripped her from my arms. I think they've missed her, but at least they got some sleep.' He sounded almost jealous and, given the fog of fatigue currently swirling around them, Lucy understood his tone. In her early days in the job, studying and working all hours, she'd thought she could never be so tired. Turned out, having a toddler thrust upon her was just as exhausting.

'I'm glad they were happy to have her. They're still grieving too. Zoe's their one and only grandchild, so no wonder. Especially after losing…' She cut herself off from forming the words she could never quite vocalise. 'I guess they'll want to cherish every minute.'

She felt him tense at her side.

'What makes you think Zoe's going to be an only grandchild? I've dated. I didn't buy the house to live alone in for ever.'

Lucy thought of her flat. She hadn't bought it to live alone for ever either. When their family home had been sold, and she and her sister had split the money, a flat had just seemed logical. Not quite a 'for ever' home, she realised now. She'd already played house, though, far before her time. 'When have you dated?' she asked, glossing over the house comment entirely. 'I never see you with anyone past the fortnight mark.'

'Well, yeah, not lately.' He fixed his dark eyes

on her, making her feel silly, on show. 'I'm not a monk, Luce.'

'Lucy,' she corrected automatically. 'And I didn't think you were, I just…'

'Since when have you followed my love life, anyway?'

'Since never. I don't care. Anyway, you can talk; I didn't know you knew about Aaron asking me out.'

His jaw clenched. 'You know what hospitals are like. Staff never have time to date; you hear things.'

'Yeah, well, I was just saying, it's good Zoe has your parents. I think it's nice your mum is able to help. She has someone that's maternal.'

Jackson's face fell. 'She has you.'

Fiddling with the strap of the handbag on her knee, Lucy looked away. 'Yeah, sure.'

'She does. You're her auntie, her mother figure, now. She'll be fine. You turned out all right, didn't you, without a mum around?'

'Oh, yeah, I'm a totally well-adjusted human being.'

His chest rumbled with a deep, free kind of laughter she'd never heard from anyone else. It always made her laugh but, as now, she'd always tried to suppress the laughter of her own that it caused. Usually, the rumble came after she'd mocked him, or been zinged by her with a clever one liner. Today was no different.

'You never thought about having a family one day?'

Until his question dropped. She didn't know how to answer—families to her meant pain, loss.

Perhaps buying my place wasn't such an impulse purchase.

'Hello!' The rapping on the car window startled them both. There was a man peering through the glass at them. 'You lost?'

'Saved by the bell,' Lucy muttered under her breath as she went to get out.

'Hey, Luce, wait!' Jackson tried to stop her, but she was already out.

'Hi,' she addressed her saviour stranger. 'No, we're not lost. My sister lives here.'

Jackson appeared at her shoulder, bumping it from coming in so hot. She looked up to give her clumsy giant companion a quick glare before addressing the man again. '*Lived* here, I mean. Can I help?'

The bloke was smartly dressed in a suit and tie. He fitted in well with the upmarket suburban backdrop. In comparison beside her, dressed like a swarthy lumberjack in his checked shirt and jeans, Jackson looked as if he'd just stepped off his country ranch. The fact the suited man had to look up at Jackson wasn't lost on her either.

'Oh, no, I actually live a couple of doors down. I'm sorry for ambushing you. I didn't realise who you were. New car?'

'No,' Jackson butted in. 'It's mine, actually.'

'Ah, right. I knew Harriet had a sister; I didn't realise you had a partner.'

'We're not together,' they replied in unison. Jackson moved a little closer. So close, in fact, he blocked her line of sight. Lucy stepped closer to the man.

'You sound like you knew Harriet.'

The neighbour thumbed towards his house. 'My wife did. We have a son the same age as Zoe. We were really sorry to hear about what happened.'

'Thanks.' Lucy's eyes flicked back to her sister's house. 'Me too.' Jackson stepped forward, putting an arm around her shoulder. She shrugged him off, flashing her best professionally honed smile at the man. 'That's very kind of you. We'll be coming back and forth for a while, so…'

'No problem; well, nice to meet you.' He put out his hand to shake Jackson's, but Jackson folded his arms in response. The man's smile dipped. 'Right, well, better go see the wife.' He patted Lucy's arm. For a second, she thought she heard Jackson growl, but when she flicked her gaze to him she saw him looking at the neighbour as if he was stuck in a boring business meeting. 'If you need anything, you know where we are.'

Lucy turned to walk towards the house when the man left. 'That was rude.'

'I know. Who is he? Neighbourhood watch?'

'No,' Lucy spat back, fumbling for the keys in

her bag. 'You jackass. You were rude then. He was only checking on the house.'

'No, he wasn't, he was being nosy.'

They got to the front porch at the same time. Lucy tried to sidestep him to get to the lock but she was met by a wall of muscle.

'Do you have to stand so close, you big oaf? I felt like you were my bodyguard back there. What did you think he was going to do—throttle me with his tie in broad daylight?'

He tutted, stepping to one side. 'No, but that's another thing.' He followed her into the house, shutting the door behind them both and looking out through the side window as if he was expecting a sniper assault. 'He knows my car; it's been parked outside enough times. The guy was just fishing. What kind of man do you know wears a suit and is home in the daytime?'

Lucy reached for the scattered letters on the mat, shuffling them into some kind of order as she rolled her eyes. Jackson was muttering to himself, his eyes glued to the window.

'I don't know, do I? We're not at work, are we? I've seen him around before, but usually I'm alone and in my own car. I don't know. I don't really care. The house is empty now. We could do worse than have a vigilant looky-loo watching over the place.'

Dumping the pile of post into her bag, she put it on a side table and turned to face him. He was still glued to the window. 'Why are you so squirrelly today? It was a neighbour. Can we please just get on with getting some stuff done here? We need to empty Zoe's room first.'

She was halfway up the carpeted stairs before he spoke again.

'I'll get the boxes from the car. Sorry, Luce. I guess I don't like being questioned.'

'Funny. You don't seem to mind asking them.'

She gripped the banister when her eyes met his. He looked so…confused, out of his depth. Something deep within her stirred, but she didn't poke at the feeling. His fear sparked hers. That surprised her more than anything that had happened in the last few days.

'You see why I am so guarded now?' she offered. The curl of his lip encouraged her to say more. 'Sometimes, the more pieces of yourself you give to people, the harder it is to keep them together yourself. You don't always get those pieces back, Jackie boy.'

He didn't reply at first, just pressed his lips together. She was at the top of the staircase when she heard him say, 'I understand. Sometimes, though, the right people keep those pieces safe because they know just how precious they are.'

She spun round, but he'd already left the house.

What did he mean by that?

She stared at the closed front door for a long

moment, before turning back and walking across the landing towards Zoe's room.

Six hours and three car trips later, they were done. Everything of Zoe's had been moved from the house, and they'd made a huge dent on the other rooms. The sight of Jackson taking apart furniture with a set of tools she hadn't even known he owned had been an event. Not entirely an unwelcome one, either. It was the first time in her life Lucy had understood the attraction women could have to a muscly man brandishing a drill. She'd had to go and get a glass of water to cool down at one point and remind herself of the reason they were there in the first place. Looking around her late sister's house had soon refocused her attention.

The kitchen had been easy enough: anything that she or Jackson didn't have went to the car. They would sell everything else with the rest of the stuff…eventually. The 'For Sale' sign would soon go up, and they'd hired a company that morning to put the rest of the stuff into a storage unit. Jackson had sorted that; he had a mate who worked there, so it had been a lot less painful than she'd first thought. They could go through the stuff later, when they were both stronger. They'd keep everything they could for Zoe, when she was older.

Lucy had taken some of the photos that were

framed, and she'd packed one that she'd seen Jackson linger over in the dining room: one of the three of them together at work. They were all looking pretty tired in wrinkled, stained scrubs. They'd worked together on a particularly hard case involving a teenager who'd come off his brand-new motorbike.

She still remembered it: the smells and sounds in the room; Jackson frantically pumping the lad's heart while she and Ronnie had raced to stop the bleeding, stabilising him enough to get him to the operating room. Hours later, when the patient was in the clear, his parents had asked them for a photo, to remember the people who had saved his life on that dark day. They'd sent the photo of the three of them standing there, by his bedside, smiling, to the hospital later. Ronnie had asked for a copy. She'd not looked at it properly in years. She reckoned Jackson might want it, and it would be good for Zoe to see her dad in action, see how close they'd all been. The thought of it being in storage gave her a pain in the pit of her stomach.

'You ready?' Jackson called from the front door. 'I thought we could ring Mum on the way, see if she wanted some dinner picking up as a thank you.'

She grabbed her bag and went over to him. Balancing the photo in one hand and her bag in the other, she fumbled around, coming up empty. 'You got the keys? I can't seem to find them.'

He waggled them at her. 'You left them in the door, Little Miss Organised. You hungry?'

'Starving,' she admitted. The sandwiches they'd had at lunch were a distant memory. Reaching for the keys, she almost dropped the photo frame. Jackson caught it. 'Jeez, thanks. I'm all fingers and thumbs.' Jackson laughed.

'I know. You're a mess.' He tucked the frame under his arm and leaned in close…so close. Lucy tensed until his hand came up and pulled something out of her tied back hair.

'Spider web,' he muttered, but when his eyes locked onto hers she could see his pupils up close. They were dilated. 'You still don't trust me, eh, Trig?'

He was close enough to reach out and touch, but the look in his eyes made her wish she were an ocean away. It was all too familiar a feeling. She'd felt it the day they'd met. Before the snarking had started.

'I trust you. I just thought you were going to pull my hair or something, our usual playground games.'

She felt his fingers brush a lock of hair back from her face, his touch along the shell of her ear.

'I was thinking about that, actually.' His voice had dipped lower, more a rumble than a voice. A sound that a woman could get addicted to if she wasn't quite so dead inside.

'You were.' She breathed, suddenly feeling as

though the pair of them were in some kind of weird bubble. 'And?'

'And I think we're a little old for the playground now, Luce. Given that we now have a kid of our own who will soon be in an actual playground, I think we should try to get along better.' He reached for another lock of hair. 'For example, it would be nice to be able to get a cobweb out of your hair without you freaking out.'

'I didn't freak out.'

'Your muscles tensed up so fast you almost snapped a tendon.'

'That's not a thing!' She laughed.

'Sure is; seen it. We have to share a house for the next sixteen years at least, Lucy. I'm probably going to see you naked at some point.'

Jackson naked? What an intriguing thought.

'Yeah! Probably… I mean, probably not. You do have doors at your place.'

'*Our* place. My point is that, if you flinch every time I come anywhere near you, it's going to get weird. Zoe will pick up on it too.' She was trying to concentrate on what he was saying, but he was still playing with her hair between his fingers. When he'd reached for it the first time, she'd seen the look on his face—as if he'd been wanting to do it the whole time. As if he was answering an old question when he touched it. She'd wondered things about him too over the years. Now, the grief was playing tricks on her mind. Yeah, that was definitely it. Close proximity broke down barriers—totally explicable.

It wasn't the only thing his words made click in her head. Zoe was probably going to pick up on a lot of things, if she wasn't careful, and their new charge wouldn't be the only one either. She'd have given the game away for sure if her colleagues could have seen her now.

His voice washed over her. 'Can we just…drop the fighting?'

That almost sounded like a plea from his lips.

'Try the whole "being nice" thing?'

Her hair was coiled around his index finger. She couldn't pull back if she tried, not that she really wanted to. Not if she was honest with herself. It felt too nice to be near him. To be close to someone like this, feel that connection.

Well, this is it, Lucy-Lu. You're going mad, acting like some kind of rescue puppy, starved for affection. If you're not careful, you'll start humping his leg.

His hand stopped moving, slowly shifting back so the hair corkscrewed free. Her silence had been too long; he'd taken it as an answer.

'Okay,' she said a little too quickly. 'I'll really try this time.'

His brows raised; he studied her face.

Why do his eyes have to be so piercing? One of life's little twists, she told herself, to make something she avoided looking at most of the time so ruddy entrancing.

'Good.' There it was, that crooked smile of his. 'You got everything?'

'Er, yeah. I thought you might like this, too.'

He studied the photo behind the glass, giving her the excuse to keep watching him, as if she could work out the path forward in the few seconds he was distracted. 'I remember this. The motorbike kid—Danny something.'

'Kirk,' she supplied. 'Danny Kirk.'

Jackson's lip curled. 'Yeah, that's him. He's actually studying medicine now. He wrote to Ronnie a few months ago.'

'That's…crazy!' Lucy breathed, looking again at the boy in the hospital bed. 'I bet Ronnie was thrilled.'

'He was.' Jackson was staring intently at the three of them all smiling in the photo. 'He said that we all inspired him that day. Ronnie was really proud of that.'

He met her eye, and the two of them looked around the hallway at the marks on the walls where the photos had once hung.

'It's weird, being here with things in boxes again. I always thought that Zoe would be driving to college from this house, you know? Taking photos in this hallway.' She pointed to the white front door. 'Harriet would have taken one of those annoying pictures, with Zoe in her school uniform—all hashtags and crying emojis.'

Jackson laughed. 'Yeah, she would.' His smile faded. 'Guess that's down to us now, eh?'

Lucy groaned and he laughed again. Tucking the photo under one arm, he took her bag with the other and headed to the door.

'Come on; I'm starved.'

Jackson's mother wouldn't hear of them bringing dinner. When they got to her house, Lucy realised why.

'Come in!' Sheila practically dragged them both through to the kitchen. Zoe was sitting in a high chair tucking into a bowl of chicken and rice. Well, she was flicking more rice on the floor than getting it into her mouth, but Sheila didn't seem to care a jot. 'I made you some dinner. Not much, just chicken and a bit of rice, some fresh bread… The fruit pies are not ready yet; I'll pack them up for you to take home next time.'

Two place settings were set side by side on the island next to Zoe. The smell of cherries and pastry filled the air. It looked as if Sheila had been cooking the whole day. There were containers stacked up on the counter, with a pile of labels on the side. Lucy was taking in the scene of domestic bliss when Sheila grabbed her, pulling her in for a hug.

Lucy had seen her quite a lot over the years at

birthday dinners she'd been dragged along to, and other family events for Zoe, or Harriet and Ronnie. She'd cried at their wedding and fussed over Jackson in his best man suit. Lucy always felt a warmth from her, an 'earth mother' vibe she'd normally baulk at. From Sheila, it hit differently.

Jackson's mother was something that she never teased him about. The love both men had for their parents had been tangible. The way the whole family spoke about each other made Lucy miss her parents all the more. Her mother and father had never seen their children as adults. Had never seen what they had become in life. Every event and rite of passage was celebrated with the usual Denning joy; she and Harriet had never really talked about it, but she knew her sister had felt it too. She had cherished being part of their clan. Their love for each other was easy even now, tinged with loss. She could see the way Sheila and Walt were caring for Zoe and Jackson—and Lucy, for that matter.

She'd never divulged it to Jackson, but Lucy always thought it was sort of cool that he cared so much about them, enjoying the time they spent together. She loved the way he hugged his mum when she reached for him next. After all, who said a man couldn't spend time with the woman who'd given him life? Daughters did it all the time and no one thought anything of it. She watched him chatting away as he grabbed a baby wipe from the pack on the island. This father thing looked natural to him, easy.

Uncle, she reminded herself. *He's always been involved with Zoe. He made more time for her than I ever seemed to be able to do.*

He was talking to his mother about the packing they'd got done, the arrangements for the movers and the storage. All while making funny faces at Zoe and picking the worst mushed bits of rice off her clothes and floor.

She didn't even realise she'd been gawping like an idiot until Sheila spoke to her.

'Sorry, what?'

Sheila shot her a knowing look. 'I was just going to say it's lovely to see you two getting along so well. Sit down—eat!'

Lucy obediently took a seat next to Jackson, her stomach gurgling as a plate piled up with food was placed in front of her. Jackson was busy tucking into his, and the pair of them sat in a comfortable silence. Sheila put even more food into various containers, checking the oven from time to time. She chatted away to Zoe, who was now de-riced and demolishing a yoghurt and some fruit.

'She's been as good as gold today; she helped me in the garden earlier. She liked baking, although some of the buns she helped with might not be fit for the bake sale at church. The flour made her sneeze on one of the batches.' She turned to Jackson. 'I saved that batch for you.'

Lucy suppressed a laugh; Jackson gave her a side-eye. 'Thanks, Mum. Glad you enjoyed it. We're back at work next week, so I'll expect more sneeze buns in my future.'

Sheila giggled. 'You do that, love. Are you sure it's not too soon for you both?'

Jackson did one of his trademark shrugs. 'We'll manage. We both have departments to run, and they're already stretched as it is.' He didn't need to mention the hole that Ronnie had left in A & E. Sheila nodded at them both and turned her attention to Lucy. 'I will look after her. I know Jackson said you were a little worried.'

Lucy wanted the ground to swallow her up. 'I never—'

'Yes, you did.' Jackson sold her out before she could finish. She kicked him under the breakfast bar. He jumped but acted as if nothing had happened. 'I told you, Mum will pick her up from nursery. She'll bring her to ours too, so that she can be in bed on time.'

Ours. Still sounds weird.

Sheila didn't show a flicker of awkwardness. It was as though everyone was just okay with it, as if they were just doing this.

We are doing this, you fool.

'If you're sure it's not too much.' Lucy tried to get back into the conversation. 'I… We…' Jackson turned his head to her, but she didn't dare look at him. 'We do appreciate all this, really.'

Sheila waved her off with a flick of her floral-patterned tea towel. 'Give over. It's what grand-parents are for. Retirement is boring at times, I can tell you. Zoe and the three of us will have some adventures.'

Lucy couldn't help but smile at the thought of that. If her grandparents had been around, her adolescence might have been easier to cope with. It was one of the reasons Harriet hadn't waited to have kids. Her parents having them later in life had meant that their own two sets of grandparents had already passed. Harriet had talked about it before she'd got pregnant. She hadn't wanted to wait.

'Family is not something to wait for,' she used to say.

Zoe would be with family she knew when Lucy and Jackson were at the hospital. Thinking about work next week was stressing her out enough—worrying about what Zoe would be doing, whether she would be happy…how the heck she would juggle work with her new life and responsibilities. 'I bet you will,' she told her earnestly. 'Zoe will love that.'

By the time Jackson's mother let them go, laden with yet more food, Zoe was tired out. Jackson could see her head lolling in the car seat on the way home, and he drove at the speed limit for once. When they pulled up at the house, Lucy lifted her out. 'I'll go put her to bed.'

Jackson put the food away, glancing at the boxes stacked in the dining room with a tired sigh. Decorating could wait, Lucy had said. The office walls were cream, the glossed paintwork unchipped. They'd taken most of Zoe's stuff straight to her room and added the rest of the boxes to the piles in the dining room. They'd deal with putting the furniture together tomorrow, which would make a huge difference to the rooms. They'd clear the clutter and help Zoe feel more at home.

There was still a fair bit of stuff to sort before their shifts started again. Work had been great about the time off, but he knew without Ronnie *and* him A&E would be stretched. Lucy's department was strong, but he knew both the staff and Lucy would be glad to be reunited. Never mind with her patients, who Lucy loved dearly. Children never saw her snakes; they got the softer side every time. He'd seen it, and he witnessed it now, watching her with Zoe.

Once everything was in order in the kitchen, he went upstairs to take a shower and wash off the day. After throwing his things into the hamper in the bathroom, he stood under the shower until he felt the hot water knead out all the kinks in his muscles. He felt it wake him up after the last few days of rubbish sleep. He felt like a medical student again, with that hazy, adrenaline fuelled way of moving through the day. When he turned off the shower, he felt human again. Wrapping a towel around his waist, he walked out to his bedroom and crashed straight into Lucy.

'What the—?'

'Oh, my God!'

His wet chest smacked straight into her face as she collided against him. Without thinking, he brought his arms up to catch her, which made things ten times worse. The towel tucked into itself around his hips fell away, just as he wrapped her tightly into his strong hold. For a second, neither said anything. Zoe let out a little cry from his former office, and they didn't move a muscle. At some point during the tussle, Lucy grappled for purchase with her flailing legs and arms and grabbed for something to steady her.

'Shh!' they said together. Listening, they both heaved a sigh of relief when they heard nothing more but silence.

Under his chin, he felt her head move up to look at him and he lowered his. Her marble-like blue-green eyes were right there, up close, wide beneath her impossibly dark lashes. His bare arms were wrapped around her tight, but he didn't move an inch.

'Jackson,' she whispered. 'My hands are on your bottom.'

'I noticed that, yeah.'

It's one of the reasons I didn't move.

She nibbled her lip, a cute little movement that did nothing to help his current situation.

'You're naked.'

'I know. I did have a towel,' he said, his voice low. 'I think you ripped it off.'

'I did *not*!' she squeaked, and Zoe made a loud snuffling noise. He gripped her tighter, just as she tightened her grip on him. 'I did not,' she said again, whispering. 'Be quiet.'

'You were the one that squealed.' He paused. 'Luce, you can take your hands off my bare bum now, if you want. I got you.'

'Oh, my God, sorry!' She gasped, pulling back. He went to grab the towel, but not before she saw…well, everything. She'd never call him Yeti again, that was for sure. He was hairless, aside from a line of thick, dark hair that ran down to his…parts…which she definitely saw a flash of before he whipped the towel back around himself. He noticed with a frisson of a thrill that her voice was breathy, almost panting—the shock, obviously. The panic of waking the toddler in the next room, who seemingly hated sleep at the best of times.

Still, a man can dream…

'I was trying to stop myself falling.'

He smirked, his chest heaving too. His breath was as ragged as the fast little puffs of air from her luscious lips. A rivulet of water dripped down his chest, running down his abs like a raindrop down a window pane. She tracked its movement as he stole a long look at her.

'You grabbed me like a squirrel does a tree.' Her jaw dropped, but when she met his eye he could see he was flushed.

This woman. She'd been in his head for five years, one way or another, a swirling tornado in his logical brain. She was addictive, maddening, enchanting, challenging.

He wondered how much he could fluster her right now. He was tempted to push it, just to see. 'It's fine, Trig. I told you we'd see each other naked eventually.'

His lopsided smile was the last thing she saw as he walked past her to his room.

'So, we could unpack some more, if you want. My vote is for a movie and a drink, what do you think?'

Those choices were not the thing on her mind at this minute. Either way, both meant being close to him for the evening.

I need a minute to recover.

'Whatever you want,' she said, trying to shrug nonchalantly. 'I'll just get changed.'

She shut the bathroom door and sagged against it. On the opposite wall, she caught her reflection in the steamed-up mirror. She saw her flushed red cheeks, the sparkle of attraction in her eyes. On her top, she had an imprint of where his wet body had touched hers. She could almost make out the ab imprints. Pulling the damp hoodie over her head, she stuffed it into the hamper.

Looking up at the ceiling, she closed her eyes. 'Harriet, if this is part of your plan, girl—it's not happening.' Taking off the rest of her clothes, she turned the shower temperature to cold.

She had work to think about, boxes to unpack, her place to sort and Zoe to look after. As the cold water hit her, she resolved to stick to the plan, like she always did. Teeny moments of attraction had peppered their involvement for so long, she was surprised she still felt them so acutely. Of course, it was easier when she hadn't been up close and personal with his butt cheeks. Wondering what was under his scrubs when she was bored at work had paled into insignificance the second that towel had hit the deck.

It wasn't the only thing hitting it, either. Breakfast was going to be awkward with a capital A. A for abs—washboard ones. She was surprised the drop of water she'd tracked hadn't sizzled to nothing.

'No, Lucy. Focus!'

'You say something?' She froze under the spray when Jackson's voice came from the other side of the door.

'No, no! Be out in a minute!'

'Okay. Meet you downstairs?'

'Yeah!' she squealed, her voice sounding strangled. 'Coming!'

She waited until she heard him downstairs and scrambled to get out. 'Coming?' She chided her reflection after she wiped the steam off the glass. 'Coming, seriously?' She jabbed a finger at her mirror image. 'That's one thing you won't be doing. Get it together!'

She needed to get back to work. She had a lot to sort out and, last time she checked, a hot, glistening wet Jackson Denning was not on her to-do list. It would stay that way.

CHAPTER EIGHT

'DO YOU THINK we should go in separately? I could hang back.' Jackson's incredulous look told her his answer. 'Okay, stupid question.'

'Yeah, pretty dumb.'

Since the naked body-bumping incident, they'd fallen into a pattern of sorts. By the time she'd settled her nerves enough to go downstairs, he'd poured out wine for them both and was sitting on the sofa, flicking through the streaming options as though nothing had happened, and that was good enough for her.

The cold shower and verbal telling off she'd given herself upstairs had strengthened her resolve a little. Her sister had just died, and her brother-in-law. She'd inherited a baby and had had to move house, one huge event after the other. He'd gone through it too, and had to watch his parents grieve for his brother to boot. Whatever tingle his touch produced was one-sided. Those long looks he'd thrown her were nothing, built up in her head, or by her surprisingly awakened libido. Whatever she'd felt in that moment, it was nothing on the scale of 'whoa' moments she'd endured. Although seeing Jackson naked, feeling his hard body up against hers, wasn't exactly something she'd 'endured' and it was not so much 'whoa' as 'wow'.

She'd been ever more aware of his presence since, in the proximity of him when they were cooking together. Passing on the landing when taking turns to settle Zoe back down to sleep. The smell of his aftershave in the bathroom, seeing his clothes in the washing machine along with hers and Zoe's.

He had looked after both Zoe and her. She'd watched them together. She'd never really bought into the whole 'man holding a child being sexy' thing. In her line of work, she saw it often, but seeing Zoe in Jackson's huge arms hit differently, put it that way.

No matter what she tried to tell herself to the contrary, she was seeing him in a new light. The trouble was, she couldn't find the switch to turn it off. She'd had a moment of what she could consider to be jealousy too, if she hadn't known better.

Over the years, she'd never cared about someone enough to feel the green-eyed monster's breath on her back. When it had happened, she hadn't cottoned on to what the sudden rush of emotion was at first, but it would have been pretty hard *not* to notice the way the nursery staff fawned over him. She was pretty sure they wouldn't be able to pick her out of a line up. They all but ignored her.

Either that or they were fluttering their lashes so fast, they missed her in their line of sight.

Making the most of being with Zoe before they went back to work had been kind of nice. She felt more at home in his house. The boxes were slowly getting sorted. The to-do list didn't feel so overwhelming. Zoe was settling down. They'd been to drop off Zoe at nursery together. They both agreed it was better to settle her back in before work schedules came into play, make things as normal as possible for her, or what was the new normal of her life now.

They'd planned to use the time she was at nursery to tackle another day of clearing Harriet's and her places out ready for the respective sale and rental ahead. She was keeping her mortgage on. She felt absurdly better with an escape plan, not that she could ever realistically use it. Still, that place was the first home she'd bought on her own. The inheritance from her parents was tied up in it. Something made her want to keep hold of it and cover the mortgage with a long-term tenant. It would even provide a little income.

Jackson had agreed it made sense and insisted that he would cover his own mortgage. She'd played the fifty-fifty card on him on that one. She didn't want to take half his house, and she wasn't going to live there without fully paying her way. He'd reluctantly given in, eventually. The compromises were getting easier as each day went by.

The easiest decision they'd come to was to take another two weeks off work together, to get things done and be there for Zoe.

Lucy found she didn't even mind that. Work was a huge part of her life, but for once she wasn't in such a hurry. The FOMO wasn't as sharp as it had been in the past. The hospital had agreed without issue, so that was that. Their time in their little bubble had been extended. Each day, the grief and feelings of being overwhelmed fell away, tiny pieces at a time.

Zoe was a source of joy for them both. Being so young, after a few weeks the calls for Mummy and Daddy had lessened, which gave them a lot of relief, but also broke their heart at the same time. Jackson's walls now held the photos from Harriet's and Ronnie's house, and he'd even come back from shopping one day with a few of the three of them together.

Lucy had barely managed to hold her poker face at seeing those. She wondered how many of them he had, how many more snaps she'd not been aware of. The paintball photo was one of them, now enlarged and framed. One was of Harriet and her on the day of their wedding, and she knew it wasn't one from the official wedding photographer. Harriet had made her look at those for weeks after the wedding, to the point where Lucy had begged her to stop.

It was a strange photo to put up, really. Harriet

wasn't even fully in the shot. Her face was hidden from view, hugging Lucy to her, and Lucy's eyes were shut tight. A tear glistened on her cheek. Why Jackson had taken that shot at that moment, she didn't understand.

She remembered the moment well. It had been after the first dance, and Lucy had stood on the sidelines and cried—not full on sobbing or ugly crying, of course, just silent little tears as she'd watched her little sister dance with her new husband. She remembered the emotions she'd had swirling through her. She could see them on her features in the photo, even with her eyes hidden behind tear-soaked lashes.

She'd felt like a proud parent, as if her child was being married off, that her job was done. She'd been beyond sad that her parents weren't there to see it. She'd wished she truly believed that they were watching from somewhere, happy that their children had turned out so well. She remembered Jackson had come to her side as she'd watched the newlyweds dance. She'd brushed her tears away quickly, folding her arms. The DJ had just called for the other couples to join the couple on the dance floor.

'Dance with me?' he'd asked, but she'd shaken her head the second the words had come out of his mouth. 'I'd rather stick pins in my eyeballs, thanks, Denning.'

'Yeah, I figured as much.' He'd laughed, passing her a handkerchief from his pocket and moving away. She'd seen a few of the guests cast admiring glances his way. She was pretty sure his dance card would get filled.

When the dance had finished, Harriet had come straight over, beauty radiating from her. She'd been a stunning bride, and when she'd hugged Lucy to her she'd whispered, 'Thank you', and Lucy had cried again.

Jackson must have taken the photo then, she realised. When he'd hung it up in the lounge, she'd lingered over it.

'Jackson, why this one?' she'd asked him. 'You can't even see Harriet's face.'

He'd just shrugged, muttering something vague and getting back to his hammering. It still hung on the wall, and she had to admit she did love it. She quite liked the house, too. They'd brought the swing set over from Zoe's old house. The more they moved around each other, cooking together, looking after Zoe, the more she felt at home—if she ignored the sizzling sexual tension she'd felt ever since Showergate.

Zoe was calmer, sleeping better than she ever had. It was nice, their little bubble. She didn't want to strangle Jackson nearly as much as she used to, and he called her Trig less and less—although Luce seemed to have stuck. She'd stopped bothering to correct him any more.

She'd started calling him Jack. Zoe's 'Jack-Jack'

was seemingly not so bad to share a life with. It was tolerable. When she caught a flash of his muscles, it was more than tolerable, in fact. She'd had a few more cold showers recently, that was for sure. She'd even taken them both to her special coffee shop after one very early morning wake-up call from Zoe.

Amy had just been leaving when they'd arrived. She'd texted, rapid-fire, seconds after leaving:

Call me! You look so cute together! OMG! It's so weird to see you getting on. We need to talk, boss!

Lucy had fobbed her off.

Whatever...see you at work!

That was going to be a conversation and a half when she got back on the ward. She still didn't know how to shut it down, either. Their worlds were merging fast and work had seemed a far-off concept at the time. Until now, when they were about to walk through the doors.

As they sat in the car, staring at their workplace, Lucy knew that the woman she'd been the last time she'd been in that building wasn't the one setting foot in there today.

'So,' she ventured, pushing her mindset back into the here and now. 'How are we going to handle this? People will ask questions.'

'Sure.' He nodded. 'HR know your change of address, though, right?'

'It's not about HR. What do we say when people ask about Zoe?'

Jackson chuckled, leaving the car without answering her question.

'Rude,' she muttered, about to get out when she realised he was walking round to open her door. 'Thanks.' He held out the crook of his arm. She shouldered her handbag, an airbag between them as they fell into step.

'People are not going to be interrogating us about the ins and outs. They'll just be happy to see us back.' His steps slowed. 'Are you wanting to keep it a secret or something?'

'No, no.' She wouldn't have Zoe be some secret. 'I'm not sure people will understand it, though. Liz in HR choked on her bagel when I called to change my address to yours.'

'Ours,' he corrected. 'I bet she did. Remember that dumb agreement we had to sign?'

Lucy smirked up at him. 'I have it framed in my office. Scares the newbies into line.'

Jackson's laugh was a loud, hearty rumble that she enjoyed just a little too much.

When they reached the foyer, he shot her a wink. 'If people dare ask, you tell them what you need to. It's our business, Trig.' Her nickname sounded almost affectionate. 'I won't say anything till you're ready. Deal?'

'Deal.'

'Have a good day.' He smirked. 'Play nice with the other children.'

Rolling her eyes, she headed to the ward.

She didn't have time to answer any questions, as it happened. The second she'd turned her pager on, she was back in A&E.

'What happened?' she asked Jackson as she panted at the nurses' station. 'I'd barely got changed.'

Seeing Jackson in his uniform was a jolt too.

Had he looked that good in scrubs before?

She never got the chance to think about it; seeing his expression had her following him to one of the trauma rooms.

'Glad you got the page. I know it was quick.' He paused behind the curtain. 'Tom Jefferson, eight years old. Partly unrestrained passenger.' His lips were tight, words clipped. 'RTA. Mother's gone to surgery already. Fractured pelvis, open femur fracture.' His jaw clenched. 'Looks like he took the top half of his belt off without his mum realising. Dad's on his way from work.'

He paused, as if he needed a minute to process his own words. 'He has a fractured clavicle, head lacerations. He had his brain and spine cleared before we got here, but he's pretty shaken up. Nurse is still digging glass out of his right side—superficial cuts, luckily. Breathe, Luce.'

She gasped, air inflating her lungs in one shuddery breath. 'Thanks,' she muttered. 'Didn't realise I wasn't.'

They gave each other a tiny little nod, as if acknowledging the moment, before they pulled back the curtain.

'Hi, Tom, I'm Dr Denning, and this is Dr Bakewell.'

Harriet stared back at her from the hospital bed, her blonde hair matted with blood. When Lucy blinked, she was gone. A young boy stared back, hair the colour of Zoe's, with wide, scared eyes. His legs only came halfway down the long bed. He looked lost, tiny against his stark white surroundings.

'Where's my mum?' he asked. His bottom lip was trembling from the effort of trying not to cry. It was enough to break Lucy out of her stupor. 'Is she okay?'

'She's going to be, Tom. Your dad's on his way.' She offered him an encouraging smile as she stepped closer, scanning his body and itemising his injuries in her head as Jackson spoke to the nurse. She heard her telling him that the glass was all out now, him telling her they'd take it from here. 'In the meantime, your mum wants us to look after you. That okay?'

Once the nurse had brought back dressings and a sling, closing the curtain behind her, he gave a slow nod.

'Good work, pal.' Jackson pointed to the equipment. 'Now you've been checked out and cleaned up, I need to dress these little cuts. Your arm and shoulder are going to be pretty sore for a while.'

'It hurts.' Tom's voice was hoarse, pained. 'I'm not going to school today, am I?'

Jackson shook his head. 'No school for a few days, but that's okay.' He leaned in, giving Lucy a chance to blink her tears away as she prepared the suture kit for his head. 'Dr Bakewell here is my friend, and she runs the children's ward. We need to give you a little sleepover tonight, but the children's ward has all the good, fun stuff.' He looked around him, pretending to be bored. 'Not like down here.'

Lucy's heart warmed as the little boy smiled for the first time, colour returning to his cheeks.

'That's right,' she agreed. 'Tom, we have all the good stuff. So, while your mum has a little rest, you and your dad can come hang out with me.' She dropped her voice to a near whisper. 'I have so many video games, you won't believe it.'

His eyes lit up. When she looked at Jackson, he was watching her, that little crooked smile matching the sparkle in his deep-brown eyes.

'Me and Dad love video games!' His little nose scrunched up. 'Xbox or PlayStation?'

'Both,' she pretended to brag. 'Now, I'm going to put some little stitches just here.' Her gloved hands gently touched the skin near his head laceration. 'Dr Denning will put bandages on your other cuts, and then we will have to put a sling on your arm to support that pesky broken bone.' She pointed at his shoulder. 'Do you know what bone you broke?'

He gave a head-shake. 'Well, it's called your collarbone.' She pointed along her own, showing him the wing-like bone jutting from her shoulder. 'The medical name for it is a clavicle, so when your dad comes you can tell him you learned all about the human body, eh?'

Another little smile came, which felt like the best reward.

Jackson leaned in, meeting him at eye level. 'Now, we need to give you some medicine for your pain, buddy. We need you to be brave, because it's a little needle, and another one in your arm.'

The little boy gulped, but sat a tiny bit straighter. 'I'm brave. Dad said when I turn nine I'll get more brave too.' He went to shrug, but winced despite the pain relief he'd already been given. 'So it's okay. I'll get more.'

Jackson's laugh felt like a balm to Lucy's triggered grief.

'Exactly.' He thumbed a gloved hand at Lucy. 'And, once you get settled upstairs, Dr Bakewell has special treats for bravery.'

Tom flashed little white teeth, showing a gap where his two front teeth had been.

'Tom?' a frantic voice called, and the curtain

swished back to show a man who looked just like the boy in the bed. His Hi Vis jacket loomed bright-orange, throwing colour into the room as he started to cry. 'Oh, buddy!' He didn't even glance at the doctors as he went to his boy and kissed his forehead. 'Oh, mate. I'm so sorry, I got here as fast as I could. Are you okay?'

Tom raised his good arm and cupped his dad's cheek. 'I'm being brave, Dad.' He eyed Lucy. 'She has Xbox and PlayStation, and she said we could play later.'

Tom's dad laughed and Lucy watched them, noting the relief on his dad's face as he laughed, kissing his boy and looking at his injuries. When she had pushed down her emotion enough to look Jackson in the eye, she couldn't help but see the tear he was wiping away with his sleeve. Clearing her throat, she got back to work.

'Mr Jefferson? I'm Dr Bakewell. Do you have a couple of minutes to have a little chat while Dr Denning stays with Tom? Tom?' She smiled. 'I'll be back soon. I just need to tell your dad how brave you are. Dr Denning will give you something to make your head feel a little bit numb, so we can get you sorted. Okay?'

The father followed her out, and she moved him away from the cubicle far enough that she could no longer hear Jackson discuss video games with Tom as he dealt with his dressings.

'I can't believe this.' The father was drip-white.

The adrenaline fading with the happy relaxed façade he'd put up for his son. 'The police called me, said he'd not had his belt on properly. He was on the way to school with his mum.' He leaned against the wall. 'I could have lost them both. They're everything. Is my wife going to be okay? Is Tom?' For a second, Lucy saw a flash of bloodied blonde hair.

It's never going to be okay. Not really.

'Doctor?'

She took a deep breath. 'Mr Jefferson, your wife and son are going to be fine. We are all here to look after you. I promise you; your family is in good hands.' She pointed to an unoccupied row of chairs along the corridor. 'Come, take a seat. I'll get the nurses to get an update on your wife.' She pointed to the foyer. 'In fact, I'll do that now for you. Go get a coffee and, when you get back, I'll update you on everything. Tom needs to stay here overnight for observations, but we can make up a bed for you.'

'Thank you.' Mr Jefferson finally drew breath. 'Coffee sounds good at the moment.'

She watched him head away on shaky legs and, calling over a nurse, wondered if Mr Jefferson would ever truly know just how lucky he was.

She was back at the funeral, standing alone by the flower-adorned coffins. There was no minister, no mourners. She was alone, and then Harriet was there. She saw her, standing at a distance. She was speaking, her lips moving fast, forming words that didn't reach Lucy's ears.

'I can't hear you, Harry! Come here! Please!'

She'd begged her to step closer to her side, past the wooden boxes. Her legs wouldn't move. She tried everything, but the grass held her feet fast to the ground.

'Harry!' she shouted, over and over, begging her sister to come closer, knowing she was saying something but not hearing it. 'Harriet, I can't hear you!' she yelled, crying with frustration. She longed to run to her sister and hold her, hear what she had to say. 'Tell me, please! What are you telling me?'

Harriet didn't come. She just kept smiling as she spoke her silent message. Lucy kept shouting, the coffins standing between them fixed points. 'Tell me!' she screamed, wishing she could rip her body away from the turf. 'Please?' she cried. 'Tell me!'

'Luce, it's ok! Stop, it's okay!'

'No! No! He doesn't know how lucky he is!' she screamed as something grabbed her. The coffins disappeared and she was in the dark, blinking the water from her eyes as she tried to focus. 'Jackson?'

'Yeah.' He soothed her. 'It's me. You're okay.'

'Harriet,' she gulped out between gasps. 'Harry was here.'

'It was a dream. Deep breaths.' Her eyes adjusted to the dim light from the landing. She was in her room, her bed, in her new home.

Home. Huh.

Her racing mind, focusing on five things at once, almost skipped over the relief she felt that she was here. The lack of shock that it wasn't her flat's bedroom walls she could see in the dim light. Jackson was stroking her arms, his bare chest rising and falling at a tempo matching hers. 'Everything's okay.'

'No,' she pushed out, unable to breathe. Her heart was pulsing in her ears, a thudding drum beat. 'I—'

'You can.' He stopped her. 'You can breathe. It's okay. I've got you. Control it. In through the nose, doctor, out through the mouth. Focus on me, Look at me.'

She pushed away the image of the flower-strewn coffins, replacing them with the dark pull of his concerned gaze. She did as he asked until the burning in her chest subsided.

He'd sensed it, the looming panic attack. Moving closer, he ran his hands down her arms one more time. He reached for the shaking hand in her lap. 'I'm here, Luce,' he'd said softly, the breath pushed out from his words whispering over her skin as he kissed the back of her hand. 'I'm not going anywhere, ever. Okay?'

She looked back at him, and the strength of conviction in his expression almost felled her. It was as though the swirling brown of his eyes was more intense, boring into her soul to bring the words home. 'You believe me, right, Luce?'

'Yes.' She nodded, squeezing his hand tight with her own. 'I know you'll stay with me.'

His face relaxed, his furrowed brow easing. 'For ever,' he mumbled, pulling their entwined hands to rest against his chest. 'For ever, Lucy. You'll never be alone again. Not while I'm here.'

The tears came soon after. He soothed her and shushed her. He brought her into his huge, unyielding embrace and lay down with her. She rested her head on his chest and fell asleep, listening to the beat of his heart.

The sun was up when Zoe woke them with her shouts, still wrapped together, her hand still caged by his, his fingers wrapped around hers. As she roused from sleep, from the feeling of waking with someone for the first time in, well, a long time, she stilled her body. She knew she had to move, but delayed it anyway. His heartbeat was steady against the shell of her ear. Neither had moved an inch the whole night.

Zoe yelled louder. 'Jack-Jack!'

When she felt him stir beneath her, the night before sprang into her head. His whispered words in the dark: *for ever.*

Oh, it was going to be another weird day.

'Morning,' he mumbled. He lifted their entwined hands, brushing a stubbly kiss onto her skin. 'You okay?'

'Yeah,' she bluffed, before she pulled away. Reality was rising faster than the sun through her window, sending her scrambling from their embrace like a startled vampire. 'I'll go get Zoe.'

'Luce?' he tried, his hold lingering before she untwined her fingers.

'I'm fine. Honestly. First day back was tough, that's all.' She sprang away from him and tucked her hand out of sight. He didn't reach for it again. His words were few after that, clipped. They went through the motions, their morning routine awkwardly stilted.

Now they were here again, back out of the bubble. Back to the normality of work. She didn't know quite how to feel about it yet. They'd dropped Zoe off at his mother's house that morning, both of his parents meeting them at the door with a tender smile. Sheila had pulled her in for a hug while the men had taken Zoe indoors with her stuff.

'Have a good day, love,' Sheila had said softly into her ear. 'You look tired. Take it easy on yourself, okay? Juggling family and work are hard enough at the best of times.'

Jackson appeared behind her, so she didn't get the chance to reply. She didn't know what she would have said anyway.

I had a nightmare? Your son is dreamy to wake up next to, and now I'm freaked out about it happening again—or not happening again?

The way she'd woken in his arms wasn't normal; she knew that much. Even without Jackson's and her complicated relationship, and their arrangement, she'd never felt like that waking up with a man in her bed. She didn't have much to compare it to, sure, but she had the feeling waking up with Aaron from the fracture clinic would *not* have felt that good, that, safe, that good. She was running out of ways to categorise it, which frustrated her all the more. She was so turned around, she didn't know what to trust. Even her gut was an unreliable narrator around Jackson.

She pushed the scramble of thoughts away, focusing on the here and now, one foot in front of the other, allowing one of her other new emotions to push to the front. Parental guilt popped its head up first, begging to be acknowledged. It had felt strange, leaving Zoe there and going off to work again. She'd got pretty used to being home with Jackson and her. Was this what working parents experienced every day? She wasn't sure she liked it. Watching Jackson at home that morning, losing his keys, spilling his coffee down his shirt, she knew she wasn't the only one affected by things.

Does he feel what I do, or is that just him being his usual caring self?

Perhaps she should have chosen Neurology. Maybe then she'd know what was going in his head.

Oh, shut up, you daft fool. Not even science can help you on this one.

They'd spent the car ride in silence. Lucy had busied herself scrolling through her phone while Jackson had grumbled about pretty much every other driver in the morning traffic.

Now they were sitting in his car in the staff parking area, drive-through coffees in hand, neither making a move to leave.

She felt his hand cover hers. They moved closer in the car, his hand still holding hers.

'You look a little tired,' she murmured. He looked away, focusing on their entwined hands. She followed his gaze and, despite herself, gave him a little squeeze with her fingers. 'I slept like a baby,' he eventually offered. His eyes found hers again, his brows furrowing a little. 'I was a little worried about you, though. I've never seen you like that. It was worse than the panic attack before. What was on your mind?'

'Just a bad dream—the Jeffersons yesterday...'

'Definitely a baptism by fire,' he replied softly. 'It got to me too.'

'I'm okay,' she assured him. 'After a bit of sleep and coffee. It's all good.'

She saw his face change, relax, and felt the relief flowing through him.

He's relieved it's not about him. He doesn't feel this tension, she thought.

The pang was unexpected. Her shields jolted to life. 'I'm not made of stone, Jackson. I know I'm difficult at times, I push things down, but I'm a wreck too.' She nudged her head towards the building before them. 'I've been looking forward to work, to getting back to some kind of reality. Moving, Zoe…everything's been so different, hasn't it? I thought it would feel easier, coming here—comfortable—but I feel sick about it.' If he wasn't going to talk about them spending the night together, then neither was she.

'I get it, more than you know. I love having you both at home. I know it's been tough, and sad, but I like having you two to come home to. You're not as prickly as you think, you know.'

Her smile was genuine then; she felt his words wash over her and her heart swelled. It was a strange feeling, but one that was happening more and more. The more she was around him at their house, looking after Zoe, fighting over the remote, it felt sort of…nice…and sexy.

Confusing! You mean confusing.

She'd fallen asleep listening to his heart beating; that had been more than sexy. It had been… more than a long-buried sexual frisson.

'I like it too.'

'You do?'

'Yeah,' she told him earnestly. 'I don't think I

would have coped on my own. I like being home with you both. It feels…normal almost, or it's starting to feel that way.'

His thumb started to move up and down the skin on the back of her hand, slow circles that made her nerve endings sing.

'I'm not as bad as you thought, eh?'

His tone was teasing, but it didn't make her her blood boil as it usually did. In fact, it made her feel a heat she'd never expected to feel. *For ever*: those words in his gravelly voice kept playing on repeat in her head.

'No,' she admitted. 'Not at all.' He was closer now; their faces had gravitated together. She could smell his aftershave, the one she had grown accustomed to in the bathroom they shared, on his skin. Heck, on her sheets now. It was all around her.

'You're not so bad either.' He breathed, his eyes falling to her lips. She licked them, feeling the air change in the car and dry out around them. 'Luce, about last night. Do you want to…?'

Her mobile rang out and they both jumped. The spell broken, she went to get it and saw the time on the dashboard.

'We'd better get in,' she told him. 'I bet that's work.' She was desperate to hear what he was going to say but, either way he went, it felt as if pain wasn't far behind. If he felt it too, so what? He and Zoe were all she had left. If it failed, it would be unbearable.

Even less bearable than knowing what could be, and not having it.

'Listen, thanks for last night.' She licked her lips again, which had gone bone-dry. 'For being there…you know, for my panic attack. It…well, it won't happen again, I'm sure.' There it was—an out wrapped in an apologetic thank you.

When she looked at him again, he was running his hands through his hair, an odd expression on his face.

'Yeah, of course.' He huffed, picking up their coffees. 'If you're sure, let's go.'

CHAPTER NINE

JACKSON DIDN'T TAKE a full breath until he got to the locker room to change into his scrubs.

What the hell was that?

Lucy had been on the phone on the walk in, giving him a coy little wave before dashing off to her department. His heart was still beating hard in his chest. A bit like the night before, when he'd lain in her bed listening to her soft little breaths as she'd slept against his bare chest. He'd lain there in the dark, cradling her and wishing he knew what was going on in that feisty, stubborn head. He'd been torn between wanting to wake her to ask if she felt a fraction of what he did and willing the sun not to rise so they could stay like that for ever.

It was harder to brush off how he felt about someone when he were in close proximity all the time. His toothbrush sat next to hers in the bathroom but she still felt like a stranger sometimes. They'd held hands until she'd woken up and shut herself away from him again, behind the snakes that had slumbered soundly in his embrace hours earlier. If he didn't know better, he and Lucy Bakewell, tormentor and tormentee, had just had a moment—a big moment. On top of many moments they'd had over the last few weeks. If that phone hadn't rung, he'd have finished that sentence.

What the hell are you thinking?

He knew what he'd been thinking. What he'd been thinking was that he wanted to ask Lucy out to dinner. He wanted to crack open those shields of hers and have her willing to let him in.

If he was honest with himself, having her at his house, their house, had been good. Since Ronnie had passed, he'd had to stop himself from feeling like it was a gift. He'd liked having her around. He fancied her, big time. She was unlike any other woman he'd ever met before, or since. She'd shot him in the nether regions on their very first encounter, and when he'd tackled her about it she'd riled him up in more ways than one.

After that day, when his pride was hurt, when it became obvious that not only did she not see him as a love interest but a rival, he'd forgotten about it. He shouldn't have entertained the thought anyway. He'd expected to meet the sister of the woman Ronnie was dating. He'd never expected to see her any other way. He shouldn't have, but he was addicted. He enjoyed the banter, the feelings she evoked within him when they locked horns. Then he'd become part of her world, her family, and it hadn't been possible. He'd brushed it off as a passing fancy, something not meant to be. The way it was possible to fancy someone one minute, and then realise it wasn't attraction at all, or something that might turn into something that would last longer than an angry, sexy, frantic screw.

He'd dated, but no one seemed to measure up. He'd thought it just wasn't his time. There'd been no deadline to meet. Then Ronnie and Harriet had passed, and he'd thought *that* was why they'd met. It was part of a cosmic plan somehow. He was meant to be there to raise Zoe, stop her being alone in the world—his brother's last wish. Lucy had just been part of the deal, and he was okay with that. Ronnie had known he could handle it, and Harriet too. He seemed to be the only one who wasn't terrified of her, who didn't step away when she pushed.

They pushed each other and made the other feel alive, passionate. The second he'd touched her hand, he'd known co-parenting wasn't the full story. This feeling wasn't a by-product of being so closely connected, or the grief. It was a primal need to have this woman. She was his. He was hooked, and he didn't even realise when his cravings had started. If her phone hadn't gone off, he'd have asked her out, told her he *wanted* to talk about last night.

Which couldn't happen, obviously. He thought he'd been more than a comfort blanket, but it was all in his addled head. They were raising a kid together, working together. If he stuffed this up, made things awkward when they were just starting to get on, when she was just starting to let him in, it would ruin everything. They had to solidify this arrangement in a few short months. Even acknowledging the logic of it all, he couldn't quite quell the irritation he felt. Maybe he should have got a clue when she'd been worried about people finding out about their new situation.

He was pulling on his scrub top when Dr Josh Fillion walked in, the doctor filling Ronnie's job. Jackson had exchanged a few emails with him, and had had an online meeting while he'd been off to get the guy up to speed on the way he ran his department. From what he'd been told by his staff, Josh was doing a pretty good job.

'Hey, man, first week back? Sorry I missed you yesterday—day off.'

'Yep.' He clipped his ID to his uniform. 'Everything still standing, that's a good start. Settling in okay?'

Josh immediately launched into what was going on and what patients they'd had in. Taking his wallet and keys from his pockets, stashing them in his locker, Jackson listened while he checked his phone. On the screensaver was a photo of Lucy and Zoe. He'd taken it when she hadn't been looking, at the local park near his house. Lucy had taken Zoe down the big slide. They were both laughing, faces happy, full of fun. He dashed off an action snap as they'd zoomed down the steel slope. It had been a good afternoon, carefree.

'That your daughter? She's cute.' Josh cut through his thoughts, bringing him back to reality. He thought of Lucy, and decided, for now, work was work. Perhaps the more separate they kept things, the less likely he'd be to lose his damn mind.

'Er...yeah.' Jackson click-locked the phone, turning the screen black. 'I'd better get out there.'

'Sure, see you in a minute,' Josh replied, turning to his locker—Ronnie's old locker. Jackson had cleaned Ronnie's stuff out himself and taken it home. He knew it wasn't his any more, but it still hit hard, as if Ronnie had never been there. He pushed his way out of the door, suddenly finding the air thin.

He could see some of his staff at the nurses' station; they all stopped when they saw him approaching. Steeling himself, he shot them a strong smile he didn't feel.

I should have addressed this yesterday.

They didn't know how to act around him.

'Hey, everyone,' he addressed them together. 'I know you all probably have things you want to say. I spoke to some of you yesterday but, since most of us are here, I'd just like to say thanks for covering, and for all the cards and stuff for Zoe, but I'd like to concentrate on the work now.'

Their faces all had the same expressions: pity,

sorrow, understanding. A few nodded, and he was grateful more than ever for the team he had under him. 'I know we all miss Ronnie, but he'd want us to carry on, kicking butt and saving lives.' He folded his arms, holding himself together when he felt as if he might come apart. The wave of grief crashed against his sand walls. 'That okay with everyone?'

One of the nurses spoke first. 'Hell, yeah.' He nodded. 'For Ronnie, guys.'

He could tell the rest of them were on board. A couple wiped at tears.

'For Ronnie,' he echoed. 'Let's save some lives, eh, people?'

As his team got back to work, and he headed to his first patient of the day, he wondered if Lucy was okay. He'd check on her later and see if she wanted to grab lunch. If this was all that being in her life was going to be, he'd just have to take what he could get.

'It's okay, Emma. Just a little scratch.' The flushed seven-year-old made a little whimper as the nurse inserted the cannula. Lucy was standing at the other side of her bed, holding her hand and keeping her steady. She had a pretty nasty infection. If her mother hadn't brought her in when she had, it could have been a lot worse. Sepsis worked fast, but it had been caught early, and getting fluids into her would help, alongside antibiotics.

Emma nodded from under her oxygen mask. Her breathing had been shallow when she'd arrived, a bad chest infection causing an asthma attack. Lucy had seen it a hundred times, but watching a child struggle for breath was tough.

'That's it, all done! It might just feel a little cold down your arm for a minute, and then you should feel a little better.'

'Thank you,' her mother said from the back of the cubicle. 'She couldn't breathe in the car; I was so scared we wouldn't get here in time.'

Lucy turned to her. 'You got her here, and she's going to be fine. We'll keep her overnight, monitor her, but she's doing great. Her oxygen levels have improved already. We'll keep her on high-flow O2 for now till they increase over ninety percent. The liquid steroids we gave her act fast, and the fluids on IV will help to hydrate her.

'Emma,' she said gently. 'I need you to be really careful with your hand here, okay? Be careful not to pull the wires.'

She read through her notes again. 'So, your GP diagnosed asthma at four?' Her mother nodded. 'How is she doing with the inhalers? Did he explain about using them with the spacer and mask?'

'I don't like my spacer,' Emma's muffled voice retorted from under the mask covering her nose and mouth. 'It smells funny.'

'She doesn't like doing it.' Her mother blushed. 'I try my best, but...'

Lucy nodded gently. 'I'll tell you what, Emma, I'll make you a deal. I'll give you a couple of new spacers with some masks attached and we'll see if they are any better. That medicine is boring, I know, having to do it every day, but it helps your lungs to work better. Especially when you get a nasty cold.'

'You've been great, the A&E doctor too. He came running over to us when we got to the main doors. He just picked her up and carried her to a bed. Will you be able to thank him for us?'

'Sure, did you get his name?'

The mother looked pained. 'Oh, gosh, you know—I didn't. He was very tall, though—huge, actually.'

Lucy continued marking up the patient file, but she felt the smirk creeping out.

'I know who you mean. I'll pass on your thanks.'

Leaving the cubicle, she pulled out her phone.

Heard you've been all heroic this morning, carrying damsels in distress.

It pinged seconds later.

Just an average Wednesday. You eaten lunch yet?

Nope. Thought I would just grab something quick later.

'K. I'll be in the canteen at one if you fancy it. Lunch, I mean.

Lucy's eyes bugged out when she saw his reply. They'd never eaten together without Ronnie…and with a side of innuendo? She began to type back.

Pretty busy… *delete*

No time…*delete*

Maybe… *delete*

Your chest makes the best pillow… *delete*

I like what your thumb did in the car… *delete*delete*

Do you feel anyt…? *delete*delete*delete*

What am I? Twelve?

She tapped the phone against her lip, wondering what the heck was going on. It was like a switch had flipped, and suddenly Jackson wasn't maddening, frustrating Dr Denning any more. Well, he was, but he was also the guy who'd held her tightly last night while she'd fallen asleep. The guy who always bought her favourite snacks from the supermarket without being asked. The huge, sexy guy who read to Zoe and make her laugh when he did the voices for all the characters. The guy who she shared a kitchen with, who whipped up more than omelettes in low-slung PJ bottoms and a bare chest she now preferred to any pillow she owned.

When they'd first started working together, she'd gone to bed particularly wound up about one of their little work disagreements and had eaten half a cheesecake before bed. She'd blamed the cheese, of course, but she'd woken up that night horny and sweaty, half-wishing it had been real. The next time it had happened, she hadn't been able to blame the dairy.

Now he was sleeping across the landing from her every night, looking all sexy in the morning in his PJ bottoms, that sexy line of dark hair disappearing under the waistband. How on earth was she supposed to bear the space across the landing now that she had the scent of him on her duvet? Something told her the cold showers and sex dreams were going to increase tenfold.

His chest. Man, his chest.

She got it now: the cliché of a body being sculpted from marble. Now she had to sit across the island from him with that chiselled temptation. All this craziness wasn't good for the environment.

How could she go for lunch with him, when

little freaky moments like that popped into her head? Zoe needed two parents, no matter what. She had to focus on that, and work; nothing else.

That call this morning, breaking up their moment in the car, bothered her. She couldn't stop thinking about what he had been about to say. Whether, if she knew, she'd be glad of the knowledge. She'd shut it down anyway, but the look on his face… It couldn't all be in her head. Surely two people would *have* to feel the chemistry between them, whether they wanted to or not?

The screensaver on her phone had come on, and she saw Jackson smiling back at her. It was a candid shot she'd taken on the sofa one night. She'd gone to clean the kitchen after he'd made dinner and bathed Zoe. She'd put the dishwasher on for the fourth time that day and had taken a bottle of wine into the lounge. They'd got into the habit of watching a TV series together, a glass of red as a reward for a busy day toddler-wrangling and sorting out the properties and paperwork of their new life.

She'd found them both asleep on the couch, Zoe laid on his chest in her little bunny onesie. Her freshly washed curls were fluffed up, her little face content. He had his arms around her, his head back, mouth wide open. She'd snapped it to tease him later, but when she'd looked at the image she'd made it her lock-screen photo instead.

'Damn it.' She huffed, bringing up his message.

'Stick to the plan,' she muttered under her breath. 'Co-parenting—no cheese.' A shiver ran down her spine, remembering his body wrapped around hers in the dark. 'Cold showers. Lots and lots of cold showers.' She started to form a brush-off text in her head, when a deep voice stopped her.

'Talking to yourself is a sign of madness you know.'

Her heart sped up as she looked straight into a pair of teasing brown eyes.

'Jackson…' She breathed far too breathily. 'What are you doing here?'

She tried for a scowl but it didn't take. His eyes dropped to the phone in her hands, his finger tilting the screen. 'I came to check on my patient. I see your phone's working.' She locked the screen, regretting it the instant the photo popped up. 'Nice photo.'

'Thanks.' She blushed. 'I thought Zoe looked cute.'

He tilted his head and gave a slow, knowing nod. 'Right. So…'

'So…' she stalled, wondering when she'd turned into a simpering idiot and how to stop it. 'About lunch,' she started, just as he finished mumbling,

'About last night…'

'Oh.' She couldn't get a full breath. 'Um… I know. It was… I…'

'All good sentence starters.' He smirked, and

she had to grip her phone tight to stop herself from kissing it off his face right there and then. 'You want to pick one?'

'I'm sorry.' She was rambling. 'I appreciate last night, but I'm fine. I… If Zoe had seen us, I think it might have been confusing for her.'

'Zoe was in her cot. Unless she learned back-flips overnight, she wouldn't have.'

'I know, but she's growing fast. Soon she'll be in a bed, and running into our rooms, so I don't think…'

The clench of his jaw told her she'd made her point.

'Got it. No more sleepovers.' He straightened up and she felt lost in the shadowy distance. 'I just came to check on Emma.'

She reached for his arm as he turned to leave. 'Jackson,' she tried.

His voice was as sharp as flint. 'I get it. Zoe comes first.' When she stared back at him, he raised his brows pointedly. 'The patient?'

Oh, yeah. He is annoyed. That sign is loud and clear.

Emma's mum was thrilled when Jackson walked in with her.

'Oh, it's you!' She rose, reaching for his hand to shake. 'Thanks for bringing him.' She grinned at Lucy before turning back to Jackson. 'I asked Dr Bakewell who you were, so I could thank you.'

Jackson shook her hand, putting his other on

top to give her a doctorly pat. 'It's my job, honestly.' He leaned down, smiling at Emma. 'Glad you're feeling better. You gave your poor mum a scare.'

'Kids, eh?' she joked, the emotion belying her easy-natured chat. 'Such a worry, but you do everything you can to keep them happy and healthy. I am grateful, to you both.'

'It's no trouble. I get it.' He sounded almost sad. 'When you have children to worry about, you have to put them first, at any cost. I have to be going, but I'm glad you're okay.'

He took his leave and Lucy checked Emma's vitals.

'She's responding well,' she told the mother. 'The nurses will monitor her closely. Excuse me.'

Jackson was halfway down the corridor when she looked. Sighing, she pulled her phone out of her pocket. The photo lit up the screen, and she fired back a message, watching as his steps slowed to read what she'd written.

See you at one.

He didn't look back, pushing the door-release button and disappearing from sight. Just as she was kicking herself for being such a chump, her phone beeped.

One it is, roomie.

CHAPTER TEN

BY THEIR FOURTH week back, Lucy felt that things were getting back to normal at work. Sure, there had been questions. Her team had rallied smoothly, accustomed to her workaholic, 'say nothing' personal work style. Amy had been there for her; she went to the coffee shop before work when Jackson was on a late shift and had child duty. Jackson told her a few people had wondered about the pair of them getting along without HR intervention, but no one asked her. She secretly suspected that they didn't dare, and Jackson hadn't said much of anything that didn't involve patients and Zoe since that first awkward lunch.

The first week was hell. They were both so tired that they barely spoke. Other than work and Zoe, they slept, ordered in or lived on Sheila's cooking that she left stocked up in the fridge. Lucy had forgotten how knackering the job was, and now she had no gym time and couldn't sleep away her days off. Not that she needed a gym; she was on her feet all day at work, running around after Zoe the rest of the time. She and Jackson got into the habit of taking her places when they were both off:

the zoo, walks in the park or soft play. All of this was a lot of fun, but none of it was exactly sedentary—no time for awkward chats or hand holding.

She had a newfound respect for new mothers. She realised just how naive she'd been, even as a paediatrician, about how hard it was, job or no job. How people had more than one kid, she would never know.

When lunch time came round, she headed to the canteen. They fell into a pattern of eating together when they could. She automatically scanned the tables for his face whenever she walked in. Even when she knew he wasn't at work, she found herself scanning the people for him.

Jackson was already there today, sitting with another doctor she'd seen in passing. They were deep in conversation; Jackson didn't even spot her walking past. Getting her lunch, she went to sit with a couple of the nurses from her ward, leaving them to talk. Since that night in her bed, she'd learned to judge his silences. Sometimes he would be right next to her but feel miles away. New people picking up on their weird tension wasn't something she relished.

'Lucy,' Jackson called to her. She smiled at her staff and headed over, lunch tray in hand. 'Come sit. This is Josh. Josh, this is Dr Bakewell, Head of Paediatrics.'

She took a seat next to Jackson, shaking the

other man's hand across the table. 'Oh! Dr Fillion; new A&E doctor, right?'

He nodded, taking her hand in a cool palm and holding it for a second too long. He was younger than Lucy had expected. From Jackson's description, she'd imagined him as being over fifty. He was a good fit, Jackson had mentioned: reliable, old school and professional. None of that seemed to fit the rather handsome hazel-eyed man before her.

'Please, call me Josh.' His brows knitted together for a moment. 'Have we met before? I swear you look familiar.'

Lucy shook her head. 'No. Well, yes—I've seen you around.' She'd noticed him in the corridor a couple of times, mostly because Amy had shown her his picture on the hospital website. She'd had a bit of a crush since she'd picked up an extra shift in A&E. 'How are you liking it?' She flicked her head to Jackson. 'Boss is a piece of work, isn't he?'

Josh laughed, flashing white teeth against the olive tones of his skin. 'He's definitely got high standards.' Diplomacy laced his words. He suddenly clicked his fingers. 'Lucy Bakewell! Of course, I've heard a lot about you too. Apparently you're a bit of a stickler for being the best.' He looked between them. 'Probably why you get on, eh?' He ran a hand along his jaw. 'Still, I feel like I know you from somewhere. Where are you from?'

'Here,' she and Jackson said in unison.

'Where are you from?' she asked, tearing open

the vinaigrette sachet in her hands and drizzling it over her chicken salad.

'Manchester, the last few years. Sussex growing up.'

'Interesting. I always thought I'd move around and work in different hospitals.'

He leaned forward across the table. Jackson moved his chair a little closer to hers. When she glanced at him, he was staring at Josh, an odd look on his face. When he saw her watching, he returned to stabbing at his food with his fork. 'Really?' Josh said, oblivious. 'Why didn't you?'

She thought of Harriet and shrugged. 'Oh, you know, it just never happened. Timing always seemed wrong.'

Josh smiled, a cute little dimple-punctuated grin. 'Well, I for one am glad you didn't.'

Jackson cleared his throat loudly. 'Josh, we need to hurry up.' He tapped his watch. 'It's busy on the floor.'

Josh looked down at his half-eaten meal. 'Er, yeah. Sure.' He winked at Lucy. 'No rest for the wicked, eh?' Jackson mumbled something under his breath, but Lucy couldn't make it out. Within seconds, the two of them were on their feet. 'It was nice to meet you, Dr Bakewell.'

She stood up from her chair, aware of Jackson watching the pair of them with an odd look on his face. 'Lucy, please. Nice to meet you too.'

'I'll see you later, Luce,' Jackson cut in sharply,

before striding off. Josh started after him, but just as Lucy was finishing off her food he came back to stand in front of her.

'Er, I don't know if you are free, but…' He fished into his pocket and pulled out a business card. 'I'd love to take you to dinner one night, if you're available?'

Wait, what?

The grip on her fork tightened.

'Er…' The business card was still in his hand, in front of her nose.

'It's just that I don't know a lot of people. Jackson's nice, of course, but he's pretty busy with his family. I thought it might be nice to get to know you better—colleague to colleague.'

'Family?' she echoed.

Oh, he didn't know. How had the gossip missed the newbie?

'Yeah, wife and kid.' He smiled innocently. 'He's always going on about them. Even has a cute little nickname for his missus—Tigger or something. So, dinner?' When she didn't answer, his smile dipped. 'Or coffee?'

'Trigger?' she checked, his words ringing in her head.

'What?'

'Trigger. The nickname.'

'Yes.' He clicked his fingers again, pointing his index finger in her direction. 'That's the one.' He laughed. 'You think I'd get it right…he's told me enough times. I swear it's the only time he cracks a smile.'

He raised himself to his full height when Jackson half-bellowed, 'Dr Fillion?' from behind him, dropping his card onto the table.

'See?' He shrugged. 'Think about it,' he said. 'Give me a call.'

Staring at the card, Lucy realised that sometimes having snakes for hair was not half-bad. Except in situations like this, when she was asked out by Ronnie's unknowing replacement right in front of the man she secretly desired. It was getting harder and harder to keep a lid on everything when the lines kept blurring.

Jackson was waiting by her car when she finished her shift half an hour late. She walked up to him, pulling her jacket around her shoulders. He took her bags from her, as he always did, putting them on the back seat when she unlocked the car with a click of her key.

'Your car's a mess again,' he grumbled as they pulled their seat belts around them. 'Crumbs all over the footwell.'

'Yeah.' She laughed, pulling the car out of the space. 'Well, Zoe had some of those biscuits she loved the other day on the way back from the park.' He huffed in response. 'What's with you? Bad outcome?'

'No,' he snapped. 'I just think that, since you

insisted on taking turns with the cars, you would have cleaned up.' He pointed to the reusable coffee mugs filling the cup holders. 'Pretty sure Zoe doesn't drink double-shot lattes.'

Lucy breathed as she turned the wheel. 'Okay, Grumpy, I'll get it cleaned out. We can take yours instead next time. What's with you?'

They were almost out of the staff car park when Dr Fillion walked towards his car. He didn't look up from his keys as they drove by.

'What did he want today at lunch?'

Awkward.

'Lunch?'

'Yeah, Luce. At lunch, when he came back to the table.' She saw his fist clench and unclench on his lap, and tried to focus on the road. 'He doesn't know about our…living arrangements. I kept your wish. Did he ask you out?'

'No. Well, kind of.'

'Kind of?'

She pulled out of the hospital grounds onto the main road, straight into heavy traffic.

'Hell. This is going to take a while; you might want to ring your parents; tell them we'll be late.'

'Fine. Will you answer the question?'

He pulled out his phone and tapped a few keys. A few seconds later, it pinged. 'Mum says it's fine, and do we want them to give her a bath? She's at ours, and said Zoe was getting sleepy.' The traffic lights turned to green and Lucy quickly took the next left.

'Tell her thanks, she just saved us about half an hour in that jam. I don't mind bathing her, though; I've missed her today.'

He tapped away, shoving the phone back into his jacket.

'Done. Did he then, or not?'

'Yes,' she relented, feeling more than a little weird about the conversation. It wasn't as if she'd expected it or flirted. Heck, she didn't know how to flirt. 'He mentioned coffee.' She bit at her lip. 'Or dinner, colleague to colleague. Do people really not know about us raising Zoe together?'

'No. You didn't want that, so I kept it quiet. Your terms, remember? So this dinner—just the two of you, I'm guessing, since he never gave me an invite.'

'Er, yeah, I think so.'

'Wow, he works fast.' The words came out like gravel. 'He only met you today.'

'Yeah, I think he's just a bit bored. You know, new town, new faces.'

'Not once has he asked me to go for a beer after work, or any of the other doctors. He can't be that lonely.'

'Why are you so mad? I didn't ask him to ask me out.' She looked across at him. He was already looking at her, his eyes dark pools in close quarters. 'I didn't say I'd go, either.'

They were pulling into their drive when he finally answered.

'You didn't say you wouldn't, either. If we're going to play this game at work, you could at least do me the courtesy of not dating my team members.'

'Games? He thinks you have a wife and kid!'

'I never told him that!'

'Well, why would he think it, then? He said you talk about us.'

'Oh, great.' He scowled. 'So I can't talk about any part of my life now? Not all of us are emotionally stunted, Lucy.'

'Oh, and I am, right, because I don't want Leeds General to know every detail of our lives? Answer me, Jackson!'

He didn't wait for a reply before getting out of the car.

'Jackson!'

He ignored her.

'Hi, love.' Sheila met them at the door, Zoe toddling along behind.

Lucy nodded to Grandad Walt, who was sitting on the sofa watching the football. He muted the TV.

'Evening, Lucy, good day at work?'

'Yes, thanks.' She scooped Zoe up. 'How's my girl been?'

Zoe babbled away, laughing when she tickled her.

'Good as gold,' Walt said, getting to his feet. 'Come on, Sheila love. Let's let them get on.'

Jackson shrugged his shoes off and headed straight to the drinks cabinet in the corner of the lounge. Clicking off the child lock, he pulled out a bottle of whiskey and a glass. Lucy saw his dad's eyebrows knit together when he noticed. 'You all right, son? Bad shift?'

He turned to see all of them watching, and he stopped pouring. 'No, Dad, all good.' He put it back, heading over to Lucy and Zoe and dropping a kiss on Zoe's little cheek.

'Jack-Jack,' she said to him, reaching out to touch his face. He kissed her pudgy hand. His gaze shifted to meet Lucy's eye and he shot her a rueful smile.

'Bath time, Zo-Zo,' he said softly, turning to his parents. 'Thanks for having her guys; you know we appreciate it. I'll see you out.'

Lucy stayed back as he waved them off. He didn't meet her eye when he passed Zoe to her. When their car pulled away, she was already upstairs. She needed the distance to cool her temper and give herself a second to process his cheap shot. She'd just put Zoe in the bubble bath when he appeared at the doorway.

She sensed his brooding presence before she saw him and kept busy, washing Zoe with her frog-shaped bath mitt.

'I'm sorry.'

'So you should be; you acted like a jerk. What's your problem?'

'I...don't think it's a good idea that you go out with Josh, that's all. I don't like it. You said we needed to keep work separate from home.'

Her hand paused as she took in what he said. Zoe lined up a duck to go down the slide.

'And I never said that I would go out with him, did I? I hardly have time to manage everything now.'

'Is that the only reason?'

'No. We work together too.'

'Hardly; he's been there weeks and you've not crossed paths till today.'

'Still, work is work. Dating a colleague never goes well.'

'Right,' he replied, but he didn't sound convinced. She could feel his pensive mood from across the room. Rinsing Zoe off, she wrapped a towel around the tot and started to dry her off. When he didn't say anything else, she looked over her shoulder, but he'd gone. A few minutes later, she heard the front door go. When she'd got Zoe off to sleep, she came down to a note on the kitchen island.

Gone out. Don't wait up. Phone is on if you need me. Jackson

'Nice.' She sighed. After showering off the day, she dragged her tired body under the covers. She'd found the business card in her trouser pocket when she'd undressed. It sat on her dresser next to Jackson's note. Picking both up, she scrutinised them. She could be stupid and play dumb. She could say that she had no idea why Jackson was mad, why he'd questioned her, but she had a feeling she knew exactly why. If someone asked Jackson out, she knew she wouldn't like it. He'd talked about them at work—his family.

His wife and kid.

It would be sweet if it wasn't so wrapped up in a big ball of messy emotional angst in the pit of her stomach. Her phone was on charge, sitting on the dresser. Pulling out the cord, she brought up the message screen and started typing.

It's me. Don't be mad... *delete*

I'm not going out with him... *delete*

Come home... *delete*

She picked up one of her pillows and threw it at the far wall.

'This is ridiculous,' she said out loud. 'What am I doing?' She looked at the photo of Harriet and Ronnie on her dresser. 'You two have a lot to answer for.'

Turning in for the night. I'll take Zoe to nursery

tomorrow. Let you sleep in and enjoy your day off. Lucy

It read a bit cold. She added a letter to soften the words.

X *delete*

Should she?

X *delete*

She hit Send before she could debate the kiss any longer. Shoving the phone, the business card and the curt note in her top drawer, and turning off the lamp, she tried to fall asleep.

When she left the house the next morning, Zoe and her backpack in tow, Jackson's bedroom door was closed. He'd read her message but not replied.

Fine, she thought to herself. *Awkward it is.*

It wasn't as though they'd never played *that* game before. This morning, she found the whole thing silly. Yeah, they'd been getting closer, but it was just the bubble they'd been in. They'd both said as much: Zoe needed stability.

It was lust, that was all. Sure, there were feelings too, but *wife and kid* kept haunting her. She tried to tell herself it was just her libido talking for the millionth time. She hadn't been near a man in, oh...for ever...and now she was living with an extra tall version of a near-perfect specimen who was good with kids, saved lives while rocking a set of scrubs and wasn't a total player. Any woman would have looked, she reasoned, and it would pass. The hand-holding tingle would stop. She'd get over the loss of her perfect night, the one where he'd held her tight and told her 'for ever'. 'For ever' was a fantasy—nothing lasted; people didn't stay. Perhaps she should say yes to the date with Josh just to put paid to this nonsense. It was easier somehow when he hated her.

'Tell me what to do, Zoe love,' she said to her niece as they pulled up to the nursery. 'Auntie Lucy is floundering here.'

'Jack-Jack,' she said with a toothy smile, and Lucy laughed.

'Well, you're a big help. Another female totally under his spell, eh?' She turned off the engine, checking her phone again. She'd texted him again that morning—for a valid co-parenting reason, of course, telling him they were low on milk and she'd pick some up after her shift. A nothing message. Still, she was sad to see that he'd not read it. Perhaps he was still asleep. She'd told him to lie in. Or maybe he was ignoring his phone because he was still mad. She'd not heard him come in the night before. Stuffing the phone back into her bag, she tried to focus on her day.

'Morning, Zoe!' an exuberant redhead said the second Zoe toddled through the secure doors.

Maddison? Melanie? Something beginning with an M.

She looked to see Lucy at her heels and the disappointment was evident. 'Oh.' She smiled, recovering too slowly to make it look realistic. 'Hi, Lucy! I thought you were Jackson. He dropped her off last week.'

'Mmm-hmm.' Lucy passed her Zoe's backpack. 'Different shifts every week. Just me today, sorry; Jackson's got the day off.'

'Aww.' She simpered, taking the bag. 'He deserves it, working so hard.' Lucy bent to give Zoe a kiss.

'Bye, darling, have fun.'

The redhead opened the interior doors and Zoe sped off to join the other kids on the carpet. One of the newer nursery staff members was reading a story to the other kids, and Zoe was a sucker for being read to. Once the door was closed, Lucy turned to leave.

'So, what's he doing today with his day off? Out with his girlfriend or something, I bet.' Lucy met her eye. Her name tag said 'Maddy'.

One mystery solved—another person who didn't know their urgent situation either.

Perhaps she should correct that on Zoe's records. They were still listed as aunt and uncle, though the manager was aware.

'Er…no,' Lucy replied, reaching for the high door handle.

'Fiancée, then?' Maddy pressed.

'Nope, not that either.' She let go of the handle, turning back to face the woman who was seriously starting to tick her off. She was too…perky.

Was everyone in heat these days?

'Can I pass on a message or something?'

Maddy's sculpted brows raised in surprise. 'Er…well, it's not exactly professional, but…'

Lucy smiled, cutting her off. 'Of course—you're right, it's not. I'll let you get on, then, Mary.' Maddy nodded, dumbstruck. Reaching for the door, she pushed it open and felt the morning air hit her flustered face. 'Have a good day!'

'Er…you too, Lucy,' Maddy called out weakly.

'Always do,' she trilled, heading back to her car. By the time she got to work after enduring the thick morning traffic, her mood was murderous.

'Hi!'

The second she walked through the hospital doors, she came face to face with Josh.

'Oh, hi, what are you doing here?'

Idiot.

Josh laughed awkwardly, pointing to his scrubs. 'Well, I work here.'

Lucy's cheeks exploded. 'Sorry, sorry! Of course you do!' She slapped her forehead with a palm. 'I haven't had my coffee yet; it's been a bit of a morning.'

'No problem,' he said with a sparkle. 'Perhaps

you should have that drink with me, tell me all about it.'

She bit her lip. She was still mad at perky Maddy, but it clicked when she saw Josh—now she understood Jackson's mood. She'd felt that way, knowing that someone was angling for a date with him. It was exactly how he'd felt at lunch the day before. She didn't like the feeling one bit.

'Listen…' She steeled herself for yet another awkward conversation. 'I'm flattered, but the reason why I'm frazzled this morning is because I had to take my…er…little girl to nursery. A little girl I share with Jackson.'

Josh's jaw dropped, his pallor at least two shades lighter. 'Oh, my God. I had no idea you were his wife.' He swore under his breath. 'Gosh, no wonder he was so moody yesterday. Why didn't he say something?'

Lucy put a hand on his shoulder. 'It's fine. You did nothing wrong. We're not married…or even together.' She took a deep breath. 'Jackson's brother, Ronnie—the other Dr Denning—he was married to my sister. She died when he did, and Zoe's their daughter.'

'Oh, my god.' Josh's face was a picture. 'I wondered why people were so weird about talking about him. Jackson's closed off, but I just thought he'd lost a brother…so it made sense. I reckoned the staff weren't talking about it out of respect for his grief, or because they were grieving too. I didn't know he even had a daughter. When I saw a photo of Zoe, he never corrected me.'

'Well, they were grieving,' she agreed. 'And it's my fault Jackson didn't say anything. He was trying to respect my wishes. But also, I'm… Trigger…and also Medusa, around here. Actually, only Jackson calls me Trigger, which annoys the ever-living hell out of me, but I'm a bit of a dragon here.' She laughed, realising that was no longer a hard fact. 'Well, I was. They call me Medusa because I'm a hard-faced tyrant—or I was.'

Josh shook his head, his cheeks reddening. 'So many things make sense now. I thought people just didn't like me or something.'

She waved him off. 'No. No, it's just a weird time. Jackson and I were sort of family, and very much work enemies. Then our siblings went and died and left their daughter for us to raise together.' She tried to wrap it up. 'So, in short—' she pointed at herself '—Medusa, Trigger. Not wife—co-carer. We live together and raise a kid.

'Listen, it's a long, very confusing story, but I'm just not dating anyone at the moment. I just needed to set the record straight. I don't want you to feel awkward at work because Jackson and I can't communicate. I'm really sorry for word-vomiting all over you, but I think it's about time people know the truth instead of skirting around me.'

'That's a lot,' he said when she'd finally stopped

to draw breath. 'Well, thanks for telling me. I'm sorry for your loss, too.'

'Thanks. And sorry again for dragging you into our drama.' She went to leave, turning back to him when something occurred to her. 'Thanks, though,' she said, meaning it. 'You helped me realise a few things. I'll see you around.'

'Does he know?' he called after her.

'Does he know what?' she asked, frowning at him.

'That you're not together,' he said, his voice low to avoid attention. 'I don't know what the deal is with you two, but I'm not sure he has the same way of looking at things you do. The way he spoke about you, that didn't sound like just a co-carer to me.' He dipped his head by way of goodbye and strode away.

She watched him leave, but didn't feel a pang of regret. His words turned over and over in her head. Lucy thought of Jackson's mood, of him being at home, all huffy. Thought of her behaviour earlier, bristling at Maddy for daring to ask about her housemate. Pulling out her phone, she rang Sheila.

'Hi, Sheila, sorry for ringing early. I'm just going on shift. Yes, yes, everything's great. Zoe's at nursery. Listen, I hate to ask, but is there any chance you and Walt could possibly do me a favour and collect her for me tonight and let her sleep over?'

CHAPTER ELEVEN

LUCY FELT EVERY step her aching feet made towards her car. Her whole body was singing with both exhaustion and nervous energy. She didn't know whether to laugh, cry or vomit. Seeing Jackson leaning against the back of her car, she didn't get a chance to choose.

What is he doing here?

She'd planned to go home and ask him if they could talk. Tell him Zoe was away for the night to give them both time to hash this out once and for all. She'd banked on the extra time driving home to gather the bravery she needed to get her words out. Spewing words all over Josh earlier wasn't something she wanted to repeat, not when these next few hours would change their dynamic again, no matter what his reaction was when she finally managed to get her words into the order she needed them.

Her heart leapt even as her steps faltered. She had to make a conscious effort to put one foot in front of the other. He looked gorgeous, which made it worse. He was wearing the soft dove-grey sweater she loved on him, the one with the

V-neck that showed off his chest. The muscles in his broad back flexed noticeably beneath the wool when he moved. She'd thought about that chest so many times that she could draw it from memory. His long, thick legs were encased in a pair of midnight-black jeans, the ones that showed off his tight behind. The first time she'd seen him leaning over the dishwasher in them, she'd had to leave the room before he clocked her ogling.

He was looking in the other direction, checking his watch, ruffling his thick, dark locks between the fingers of one hand. Seeing the tension in his gait, she braced herself for what was about to happen.

'Hey, you.'

He pushed off the car, levelling her with one look.

He's absolutely stunning. How the heck have I ever been around you and not been a gooey mess?

'Hey. Hi.' He stepped forward, making her feel smaller as he stood close.

Not smaller—dainty.

He reached for her work bag, and she gave him it to him readily. 'Good shift?'

'Not bad.' She breathed, willing her body to stop feeling as if it was on fire. Her heart was thudding in her chest cavity, so loud she felt he must hear it. 'What are you doing here?'

He pointed to his car a few spaces away. She'd not even noticed it.

'I thought we could take a drive. Talk.'

'What about my car?'

'Leave it here. I can bring you back after.'

Well, this is not my plan, she thought, but he obviously had things to say too. It wasn't as if she'd expected anything different.

'Luce,' he mumbled, so close to her now she could have reached out and touched that legendary chest. 'You trust me, right?'

She almost laughed at him. It was such a daft question now. She trusted him more than anyone else in the world. 'Of course,' she said instead.

'Then come with me,' he urged, his voice deep, pleading. He held out a huge palm and she put her hand straight into its grasp.

He pulled out of the car park and headed away from the direction of Zoe's nursery.

'Where are we going?' she asked, looking at the buildings going past as he drove in the opposite direction from the city centre.

'That trust thing didn't last long.' He smirked. 'I spoke to my mum, by the way.'

'Oh, really?' she said nonchalantly. Her squeaky voice didn't get with the program. 'Is she okay?'

'Thrilled to have Zoe for the night, yeah, which is why I didn't drive to the nursery earlier to get her.' He turned to look at her as they hit the motorway turnoff. 'You didn't say why you wanted the night off, though.'

Zoe felt her cheeks get hot. 'Is that why you came to work—to check up on me?' Something else occurred to her. 'Did you think I might be going out with Josh?'

'It crossed my mind.' She didn't miss the clench of his jaw. 'But I spoke with Josh. He called me about a patient, mentioned he was going out with some of the team.' He cleared his throat. 'I might have suggested some of the work lads take him out for a drink—welcome him properly. You don't have any plans, do you.' It was a statement.

'No,' she replied.

'Thought so. I thought you might want to talk too, so I came to get you.'

'So you did all that and came to stalk me in the parking lot. Nice.' He laughed when he saw her knowing smirk.

'Well, I didn't want to risk the chance some other doctor asked you for a date before you got home. I didn't want to wait to see you.'

He took the next turnoff. They were on the outskirts of Leeds, she noticed, where a large retail park and some industrial units stood. 'And now you're taking me to the warehouse district. I know we sorted the joint life insurance, but I'm pretty sure murder voids the policy.'

'Hah-di-hah!' He headed to the bottom of the main industrial park, turning off just after a bathroom wholesaler. 'I just wanted to talk to you.

We've not spoken since yesterday, I wanted to clear the air.'

'You weren't talking, actually. I sent you messages.'

'I got them.'

'I know.'

He pulled into the car park of a grey warehouse. Neon lights lit up signage on top of a large set of double doors. 'I was mad.'

'Yeah, and you're weren't the only one, Jack.' She looked at the name of the place: *Axe Me Another.* 'Where are we, anyway?'

He turned off the engine, pinning her with a grin so cheeky and so sexy she wanted to slap him, then pull him in and snog his face off.

'Well, since you bagged us a night off, I thought that we should do something about being mad with each other once and for all.'

'You've got to be kidding me.'

Jackson was positively gleeful as he passed her a set of overalls. She looked up into his eyes and they were bright with excitement.

'Nope.'

'You're an A&E doctor. You put people back together after dumb accidents like this.' They were in a side room, having just signed a bunch of disclaimers and been shown where to change. Jackson shrugged, pulling off his sweater without warning. Lucy squeaked, turning to face the lockers on the other wall. 'Jackson! What are you doing?'

'Getting changed! Come on, don't be a priss. It's nothing you haven't had hold of before, remember?'

Remember? Ha! It's etched onto my grey matter.

'How could I forget?' She sighed, looking again at the bright-orange jumpsuit and goggles in her hands. 'Fine. If we must dress up like hardened convicts, at least turn around.'

She heard him behind her, closer than before. 'I promise not to peek.' He half growled; his voice sounded strained. She looked over her shoulder; he was standing with his back to her and his stance was taut. She turned round and got changed as quickly as she could. Then she tapped him on the shoulder and he turned round, goggles on the top of his head like a pair of shades.

'I look ridiculous,' she told him. 'Orange is definitely not the new black.'

He laughed with that low rumble that did things to her insides.

'I like that laugh.'

His brows raised in surprise. 'Thanks.' His smile was genuine, bashful even. She went to push a lock of hair away from her face and he beat her to it, curling it round his finger before sweeping it behind her ear. 'You look cute in orange.' He paused, and she stood there, looking up at him and prompting herself to breathe. 'Come on,' he muttered, breaking the spell. 'Let's go get that rage out.'

Half an hour later, Lucy was throwing axes like a pro. The whole place was a rage-relief experience. They had a rage room full of stuff such as china, bottles, old furniture and weapons like bats and golf clubs. She could hear people screaming and bellowing from the other rooms, and the smashes and crashes. Their space was like a shooting range with big targets on wooden walls, and axes laid out for throwing.

'There you go, Luce!' Jackson hollered as she sank another axe into the target, this time almost on the bull's-eye. 'You nailed it!' She turned to see his palm up, and high-fived him as he laughed. 'Feel better?'

'Well, I'm not mad any more.'

I might have imagined Maddy on a couple of the throws, though.

He chuckled. 'Good. We should come again.'

'We should join up to their loyalty scheme or it might get expensive.'

He laughed, that rumble giving her a tingle under her overalls. 'Hungry?' he asked.

'Starving,' she answered.

'Let's go get something to eat,' he said, putting his arm around her shoulder. They put down the axes and headed back to the changing room. They were the only ones there, and Jackson clicked the lock on the door. They stood behind the door for a moment, toes almost touching, suddenly feeling awkward after the chaos.

'Why did you come to meet me at work?' she asked him. 'Why didn't you just ring me?'

'I thought you might ignore me, after yesterday. When Mum said you'd asked her to have Zoe, I connected the dots. I found this place online a while ago and thought it would be good to have some fun for once.'

'It was.' She grinned. 'Especially after this morning.' Her eyes widened. She hadn't meant to say that.

He lowered his head closer to hers. 'This morning?'

'Er…yeah.' She shuffled from foot to foot. 'I spoke to Maddy.'

His expression was blank, which cheered her up to no end. 'Maddy who?'

'Maddy, from nursery?'

He shook his head, his lip curling into a 'so' motion. 'And?'

'And she wanted to know if you were spending the day with your girlfriend.'

She could have sworn on the medical textbooks she revered that his eyes lit up.

'Ah. Right.' He grinned, all lopsided smile and pearly white teeth. 'You were jealous.'

She flushed, the fear of being so close to him

scaring her. She didn't just mean body to body either. 'No, of course I wasn't.'

'Liar.'

'Jackson, come on.'

'No, you come on, Luce.' He sighed, thumbing towards the door. 'We did the rage. I'm not doing the denial thing any more. I was jealous.'

'Of Josh?'

'Yeah.' He huffed, taking a step closer. 'I swear, I wanted to fire the guy on the spot. I saw him hand you his card.' He bit down on his bottom lip and she tracked the movement. 'I didn't like it. I don't want you to date him.'

'Yeah.' She raised her chin a little. 'Well, I saw Josh this morning.'

There it was again—that low, reverberating growl.

'I set him straight—told him the truth and that I won't be accepting any invitations from him.'

'You did?'

'Yep. I will not be dating Josh, so I don't want you dating Maddy.'

'Done. I don't want you dating anyone.'

'Done,' she shot back. 'Same goes for you. What else did you want to talk about?'

They were both breathing a little faster now, moving infinitesimally closer.

'Why you arranged for Zoe to sleep over at my folks'.'

'Because I wanted us to talk without distractions. Why did you really come to meet me in the car park?'

'Because I couldn't wait to see you a minute longer.' His lip twitched. 'I meant it. I didn't want someone else hitting on you before you got home and I got the chance to tell you that you drive me crazy.'

'You drive me crazy.'

'I know.' He growled. 'But you drive me crazy more than when we fight, Luce. I…'

He sighed, a bone-shattering, deep sigh as his arms came up around her. She put her hands on his chest and he stilled, as though she was going to push him away. When she didn't, he went on.

'I can't lie to myself any more. I won't. Fighting with you is the most alive I have ever felt. You get under my skin so badly, I want to unzip it and tuck you in. Since the paintballing day, you were it. But I knew Ronnie and Harriet were end game; it was too complicated to even try. I thought you hated me, too. So, I told myself it was fun, sparring with each other, picking fights, and it was—but I can't sleep across the hall from you for much longer without losing my mind.

'I spent the night in your bed, and now I can't stop wanting it again. I just lay there, holding you, smelling your hair and wishing I could wake you and chase those bad dreams away *for ever.* I started using your conditioner just so I can smell that coconut smell you had that night; I need it with me when I'm away from you and can't get my fix. I can't afford the damn water bill any more, with all the cold showers. That day, when we crashed into each other, I barely got out of that alive, Luce. I wanted to just pick you up and carry you to my bedroom.'

She heard her breath hitch in her throat.

'I want your hands on my bare ass *for ever.* I swear, it took everything I had in me not to wrap your sexy legs around me and take you to my bed.'

'Why didn't you?'

Lucy was so turned on, she couldn't stand it. His words were like caresses she'd wrap herself in. *For ever...* Every time he said it, she wanted more, wanted to tell him yes. To beg him to do all that, and more.

'Because you weren't where I was. Because you pretend to hate me. Sometimes, I think you really do.'

'I don't,' she rebutted. 'I've shampooed my hair so much since we moved in together, I think my hair might fall out. The other day you were taking the rubbish out and I wanted to wrap myself in a bin bag just so you'd lift *me* up and throw me over your shoulder. You wind me up so much, I can't stand it. I don't hate you Jackson, I have cold showers too, to stop myself from blurting out how freaking gorgeous I think you are. Then I think about you *in* the shower, and I forget I washed my hair already, so I do it again. Then I smell your shower gel on the shelf next to mine and the whole cycle starts again. Even when we're with Zoe, my mind wanders. I can't help but notice how sexy you are when you're being cute with her.'

At some point when she'd been talking, he'd tightened his grip on her; her feet were barely on the floor now as he held her to him. She could feel him breathing hard, almost panting beneath the orange jumpsuit.

'I'm not stupid, Jackson. I know I'm a mess, and stubborn and prickly, but I swear, when Maddy asked about you this morning, I got it. I know why you were angry about Josh.'

She bit her lip, afraid to say the final thing she had to tell him. She felt it would be too much, she'd be too exposed. And far too turned on to concentrate on the dull panic her rational brain was trying to convey down her frazzled nerve endings.

'Because...' Her voice gave out. 'Because it's not hate, or lust, it's...'

'Because you're mine,' he answered for her. When she nodded, he lifted her off the floor into his arms, and she wrapped herself around him as he leaned her against the door and pressed his lips to hers. 'Finally.'

Oh...this man is going to be the end of me, she thought as she tasted him for the first time.

His lips were soft at first, as if he was waiting for her to come to her senses. The second she moaned into his mouth, all doubts were gone. He kissed her like a starved man, as if he'd been waiting his whole life to caress her mouth. 'Lucy. You're…so…mine,' he rasped out, his voice all growly.

'Shh,' she said, threading her fingers through his hair and pulling his mouth back to meet hers. 'No more talking.'

She felt his little laugh and she wriggled closer to his body. The laughter stopped, replaced by a visceral rumble as he ground her against the door. Sexual tension years old was unleashed. She grabbed his zip, pulling it down. His torso was bare, and she pulled away from his mouth to marvel at it. 'I love your chest,' she murmured as his lips fell onto her neck, nipping and kissing along the length. She leaned down and took a nipple into her mouth, licking at it and feeling the sensations in her own groin.

'Are you trying to kill me?' he mumbled, lifting her higher as she reached for his zip.

'Yeah,' she panted. 'Death by sex.' The orange jumpsuits were getting hot; she felt her body roasting from the inside. 'Take it off,' she begged.

He met her eye, and she could see it was taking him everything to slow himself down. 'Are you sure? We haven't talked about…'

She was already pulling at her own zip. 'Jackson,' she begged. 'No talking.' If they started talking about this, what it meant, she'd sober up from her lust. She was drunk on him, and she didn't want to stop. 'Take off your clothes. Now.'

One minute she was pressed up against the door, the next she was on her feet, her breath ragged, loud, in the room. He undid his zip the rest of the way, leaving him standing there in black boxer shorts.

She shuffled out of her jumpsuit, leaving herself in her underwear. The dark hue of his eyes deepened as she looked back at him shyly.

'Oh, no, not the green…' she heard him mumble. Looking down at her matching jade underwear, she started to pull her clothes back up, but he stilled her with his hand, picking her up once more.

'Don't you dare,' he warned. 'I just meant I knew I'd be lost when I finally saw you in them.' His teeth found her nipple through the lace as his body covered hers once more, leaning against the wooden door, overalls discarded. 'Ever since I found them in the dryer, I've been obsessed with the colour green.' He sucked gently, and she gasped as her nipple hardened beneath the lace. Pulling his head back up to meet hers, she wrapped herself around him tighter. She was desperate for him to do more, touch her more, say more.

'Stop teasing me, Denning,' she begged. This time, when their lips met, neither of them spoke. The dam finally broke between them and they were all hot breath, fingers, pulling and pushing. She clawed at his back. He was everywhere all at once, tongues and teeth, skin on skin. He groaned when his fingers finally dipped below the lace, and then he shifted her in his arms.

'I'm about to get a condom…' He panted, his arms solid around her quivering body. 'Last chance to stop this, Luce. We need to…'

She pushed her finger to his lips. 'Get it,' she begged. 'Don't stop now.'

She ground against him. 'Sex now. Talk later.'

His eyes darkened and, when his lip curled up, she knew who the victor was. Not letting her loose, he grabbed a foil packet from his jeans and passed it to her, only releasing her to drop his pants. Hers followed suit. Rolling it on, she felt him stiffen in her grasp, and then she was back in his steel hold. He kissed her frantically, pinning her to the door and lifting her legs higher. He told her to hold on tight and then he was inside her, thrusting, teasing and hitting everything just right. She was flush against the wood, limbs clinging to him as he started kissing her.

Why the hell weren't we doing this the whole time? she thought as his hot length speared her harder, deeper, hitting the sweet spots she dimly remembered and some she'd never known she had.

She tried to be quiet, aware that she could hear shouts of rage coming from behind the door, so at odds with the sounds of pleasure from within. He took every moan she had and muffled it against his jaw, against his mouth.

'Lucy…' He breathed. 'You feel so good. Lucy, my Luce…'

His movements were faster, more erratic, as she tightened around him. When he whispered her name again, she was done for, toppling over the edge as the white-hot orgasm ripped through her body, but still he drove on. Thrusting and cradling her to him as if he couldn't bear not to touch every inch of her, he growled and she felt him come hard. His arms came up under her bare bottom like a muscular shelf, holding her steady as she felt him shake on his own legs. He kissed her again and then touched his forehead to hers. Coming back down to reality, they both looked into each other's eyes, still wrapped around each other, sweaty and glistening.

'I guess that's what they mean by make-up sex.' She giggled. He huffed out a laugh, kissing her forehead and flashing her a smile she'd never seen before.

'A few years in the making,' he mumbled, before his expression turned serious. 'I meant what I said—you're mine, Lucy.' He kissed the corner of her mouth, and she felt him tighten himself around her protectively, as if he was afraid she'd bolt from his embrace. 'If you'll let me, I promise to make you happy—you and Zoe. I can't bear to go back now. Not now I've had this.' His look turned positively feral. 'Had you. There's no other woman on this planet who drives me insane. No other woman I'd rather be with.'

He kissed the opposite corner, turning her in his arms as he carried her away from the door. She wrapped her arms around his broad, sexy shoulders. 'What do you say?' He looked so nervous, so utterly gorgeous, her mouth went dry just looking at him. 'I'm pretty good at reading you, Luce, but I need a clue here.'

She leaned forward, brushing her lips against his. 'I say I'm ravenous.' His hopeful grin dipped, and she couldn't bear it. The bubble they had was thicker now, and she didn't want to pop it. 'Take me home, Jackson. Feed me, and then you can take me to bed and show me just how much you mean all that.'

His face split into a devilish, delirious smile and he twirled her round as he spun on the spot. 'Jackson!' she squealed as he bellowed out a whoop. 'People will hear you!'

He put her back on her feet, reaching for his clothes. 'Let them,' he said, slapping her on the butt cheek as they both scrambled to get dressed.

That was the last night they slept in separate rooms. He kept good on his word. He drove her home right away and fed her appetites until she was satiated. He showed her how much he meant every word, more times than she could count.

Much, much later, he curled her into his arms, smelling her hair with a contented sigh as they cuddled in her bed. As she felt her heavy lids close, lulled by the sound of his heart under her, she smiled as he whispered more words to her.

'I want to sleep like this for ever, Luce. There's no getting rid of me now. I love you.'

Lifting her head, she saw the nervousness in his face as he stared back.

'I do. I love you.' His grip tightened, just a touch. 'Don't run. I haven't the energy to chase you right now.'

She laughed softly. 'Where would I run to?' she asked. 'I'm home.' She kissed him, wanting the little furrow in his brow banished as he waited to see her reaction. 'I love you too, Sasquatch.'

His returning grin was her new favourite thing, she decided, before sleep won.

CHAPTER TWELVE

IT HAD BEEN going so well—*so well.* The sex was hot…more than hot. It was as if the pair of them were teenagers. Since the Axe Me Another frantic bonking incident, as Jackson affectionately referred to it, they'd never stopped. They'd christened all the rooms in the house bar Zoe's. The shower was Jackson's particular favourite. He loved to soap up her boobs while they stood under the spray, he turning the shower to cold to shock her just after they'd heated each other to the point of combustion. Name anywhere, they'd done it there: her car; his car, twice. There was even a stack of mops in the downstairs cleaning closet that was still blushing.

It wasn't just the sex, though. They were together in every sense of the word. Jackson was romantic, which she'd never expected but readily appreciated. He'd leave her little notes around the house, stuffed in her locker at work or in the lunches he made her take to work in case she forgot to eat—which she did, of course.

I always called you Trig because it was our thing. A reminder of when we first met.

You're such a good auntie. Zoe and I heart you mucho.

See you tonight, baby, miss you already.

Eat your greens, Dr Bakewell.

Their work colleagues were surprisingly unshocked. When she'd told Amy, she'd just laughed. 'I knew it,' she'd said. 'About time mate. Man, it's so good to see you happy.' Lucy had laughed, wondering at how things had changed.

They'd had an offer on Harriet's and Ronnie's house; a young couple had offered the asking price. She'd even found a tenant for her place. She hadn't told Jackson yet, but she reckoned that, after the lease expired, she'd sell up too. There'd be no point in having the place, and she no longer thought of it as home.

Zoe was thriving too, growing every day. She talked more and more all the time. She loved living with Jack-Jack and 'Luby', as she called her. Lucy had worried about whether the pair of them together would confuse her, but she didn't seem affected. In fact, she seemed thrilled to see the pair of them together. Jackson told her it was because kids were smart, and happy parents meant happy children. It was true, she came to realise as the days went on: they were all really happy. She should have known it wouldn't last *for ever.*

It was a Friday like any other. They were both on the late shift, Zoe sleeping over with Sheila and Walt, who were doubly elated at the news that Lucy was now even more part of the family than before.

I can't wait to sleep in tomorrow...shattered. Then I'm going to do that thing that makes your toes curl. Then breakfast. I'm thinking of pancakes at that place we like after we pick Zoe up.

Lucy laughed to herself, tapping out a response as she sat in the break room, resting her tired feet. She had five minutes left on break, and a ton of paperwork to get through. There were also a couple of patients she wanted to check on before she left.

Sounds good. I love pancakes. And you.

He typed back almost instantly.

Don't play with me, woman. Or I'll do it twice. With more tongue. Love you too.

She almost choked on her coffee. It was criminal how sexually combustible this man made her. She couldn't get enough of him. Harriet and Ronnie wouldn't be in trouble when she finally saw them again, that was for sure.

Promises, promises. See you soon.

See you soon.

A second later, another message popped up.

I'm going to marry you, Luce. Real soon.

What?

She read the words again and saw that he was typing again. She held her breath, waiting for him to take it back.

He wants to marry me? No. It's too soon. It's... too much. She was an aunt, a carer, a lover. She was his...but wife? Harriet had been a wife, their own mother too—look how they turned out.

Her old shields, stiff from lack of use these last few months, clanged back into action, raising up around her with a rusty screech. She felt her heart race as she saw the three dots bounce in the corner. He was still writing.

Don't freak out. We can talk later.

Talk later? Seriously? He'd told her something like that on a text and then expected her to work the rest of her shift? Her head was an utter mess. She wished that she didn't react this way, that she didn't want to run, but the second she'd read that text with their six-month review looming… It was too much. It felt like too much. She needed things just to slow down. They were about to cement their care for Zoe, which was a formality, but still. Marriage was binding: *for ever.* That suddenly felt like a threat, not a promise.

She tapped back.

You bet your ass we will.

His reply was instant.

Are you annoyed? I'm sorry, I know I should have said it to your face, I just couldn't hold it in any more. We'll talk tonight, okay? I have to go. A&E is slammed. Trust me, Luce. You said you were done running. Love you.

Fine.

That was all she could bring herself to write back. It felt as if he'd dropped a bomb at her feet. What should she do—run, seek cover, throw it away? The old Lucy would have without a second thought with not so much as a glance over her shoulder. He knew that. He'd dropped a grenade, and she was standing there, left to stare at it, knowing in all probability it was going to detonate and take off her face. She *was* angry. He was ruining it, changing things. They were going well, doing okay. Surely they could just go on as they were? Why change anything?

In a couple of days, after the six-month review, they were going to tell Sheila and Walt they were thinking about adopting Zoe. That was spinning her head already. Yeah, she wanted it, but it felt so final. Marriage would mean something else to risk losing. She couldn't take any more pressure. He loved her—*loved her.* She should be happy, right? She loved him. That hadn't and wouldn't change, but things were good as they were.

She cared about him, a lot. She loved waking up with him every day, sharing a bed. Falling asleep listening to his heartbeat was one of her new life's pleasures. She finally understood what Harriet had been on about. She got it. She was in this, but it was still so new, so precious, so fragile. They were exclusive, raising a kid under the same roof. That was commitment, more than she'd ever given anyone. More than she'd ever thought she would. She didn't want to go back to sleeping across the hallway.

Then she thought of what came next after someone said the 'M' word. They already lived together, but that was part of the arrangement for Zoe. It had lessened the blow of their grief, and had been a necessity. It had been thrust upon them, but now—this was different. It would be on them. If this next step failed, if she couldn't give him what he wanted, what then? 'For ever' was a long time, and look where it had got her sister and her parents. The one thing she'd learned was that love did not conquer all.

She saw the time on her phone and cursed.

Looks like my break is well and truly over.

Putting her phone back on silent and shoving it into her pocket, she speed-walked back up to the ward.

When rounds were over, Lucy headed for her office.

Nearly there, she told herself as she reached for the handle. *You can hide out here, do your paperwork. Catch your breath.*

'Dr Bakewell?'

So close.

Amy fell into step alongside her, following her into the room and taking a seat opposite hers.

'Well.' Lucy huffed. 'Come right in.' She slumped down in her chair. Amy was glaring at her from across the desk. 'What?' she snapped.

'Exactly. That's what I want to know. What's up? You've been like Mary Poppins lately, and today you've been biting people's heads off.'

'I have not!'

'Yeah, you have. None of the other staff dare mention it, but you've been worse than your old self—Medusa with a side of mean. What's going on?'

Lucy clenched her jaw and started shuffling papers on her desk.

'I'm not going till you tell me.'

Lucy tried to stare her down, but Amy just laughed. 'Nice try, mate. Your snakes don't scare me.'

'Fine.' She put down the papers. 'First of all, Medusa is better than Mary Poppins, so that's a rubbish insult. Second, I'm okay.'

'No, you're not. So, what's going on? Is it the adoption thing?'

'No. Yes. I don't know.' She bit the bullet. 'Jackson just told me he wants to marry me—by text.'

Amy's eyes bugged out.

'Exactly—you get it. It's bad, right? I mean—what is he thinking?' When Amy didn't answer, Lucy looked at her expectantly. 'Seriously, tell me—what is he thinking?' Her friend smiled with a slow, knowing grin. 'Why are you smiling?'

Amy leaned forward, resting her elbows on the desk. 'I'm thinking that for a smart, driven woman, you're pretty dumb.'

'Oh, well, thanks! I—'

'He told you he loves you because he does. He told you he wants to marry you because he does.' Her eyes narrowed, a look of wonder crossing her features. 'You really don't see it, do you?'

'See what? How soon this is? How crazy?'

'Love is crazy, Lucy. What you have been through is nuts. Anyone else would have crumbled, but you two—you make each other stronger. That man has hankered after you ever since he came here. The whole hospital can see it, and you really can't?'

'No.'

'Still?' Amy's tone was incredulous.

'No, I mean I can see it.' To her horror, a tear slipped down her cheek. She stopped its descent with a shaky hand. 'That's the problem. It's not just my life—it's three lives. I don't know how to do this, Ames. I never wanted to be in something like this, something that I could stuff up. I could lose it all. Nothing good ever stays. We were fine as we were.'

They were interrupted by a sharp tap on the door. 'I'll get it,' Amy said softly. After talking to the nurse, she closed the door again.

'There's a consult in A&E. You want me to take it?'

Lucy was already on her feet. 'No, I'm good.' She wiped her eyes. 'Do I look okay?'

Amy took a tissue from her pocket and rubbed at Lucy's cheek. 'You're good.'

'Thanks.' She smoothed down her uniform and fixed her hair. 'Tell the staff I'll try to keep the hissing to a minimum but, if the name Poppins is used in the same sentence as my name again, all bets are off.'

She was halfway out of the door when Amy spoke again.

'Being scared of losing something is normal, you know. Not reaching for what you want in case the worst happens is all well and good, but it's not a life either. I don't want that for you, mate. Not now, when you've seen how great it can all be. You've lost enough already. You didn't have a choice then. You do now. Life is fleeting, just like happiness. You have to go for it while you can.'

'Hey!' Josh greeted her with a wide grin. The place was rammed, the staff rushed off their feet—a typical Friday afternoon. 'What brings you down here?'

'Paeds got paged. One of your patients?'

He shook his head, nodding to Triage Four. 'In there.'

Jackson was standing by the bed when she got there, suturing an arm laceration.

'Hey.' She didn't look at him for long, but she felt his eyes watching her as she introduced herself to the teenaged patient. 'Hi, I'm Dr Bakewell. How are you feeling?'

'Pretty rough,' the teenager croaked. Aside from his arm lac, he had two black eyes forming, an obviously broken nose and a rather nasty lump on the side of his head.

'This is Lachlan, fifteen.' Jackson told her. 'Came off his skateboard at the top of the slope at the skate park. Ambulance brought him in, parents are on the way. I sent his friend to go get a drink.'

'He's scared of blood!' Lachlan laughed. 'Ouch.'

'Try to stay still,' she urged, shining a torch into his eyes. 'Normal pupillary response; did he stay conscious at the scene?'

'Ambulance said he was when they arrived but his friend Joe said he did knock himself out.'

Lucy nodded, checking his chart. 'Let's get him a head CT. No broken bones.' She donned gloves, removing the gauze to check his nose. It was cut on the bridge, the skin split but intact. 'Landed on your face, eh? Did you land the trick?'

Lachlan grinned. 'Yeah, stacked it straight after, though. My board broke on the railing.'

'No helmet either,' she chided, inspecting his head. He had a cut in his hairline that had already been glued. 'Do I need to lecture you about being safe over looking cool?'

Lachlan groaned. 'No. My mum always tells me. She's going to go mental when she gets here.'

She locked eyes with Jackson. 'Parents worry. I'm pretty sure she'll just be happy to see you, know that you're doing okay.'

She saw his eyes soften, and returned to Lachlan's face. 'Let's get you up to CT; we'll make sure your head injury is okay. Your nose is going to need some TLC, and you'll feel bruised and battered for a while.' She applied fresh dressings as Jackson finished sewing up his arm. Noting her instructions on his chart, she motioned for a passing porter to come over. 'Once we've done that, we'll get you up on the children's ward.'

'I have to stay overnight? Aww, man! The footie's on tonight.'

Jackson cut in. 'Leeds fan, eh? Good man. Your room will have a TV. We have that channel.'

'Safe.' Lachlan held out a fist, and Jackson bumped it gently with his gloved hand.

'I'll see you soon, Lachlan.'

Jackson was hot on her heels when she left the cubicle.

'Lucy, wait.'

'It's busy, Jackson, we can talk later.'

He blocked her path, taking off his gloves and shoving them in the adjacent bin. 'Fine.' He headed to the sink to wash his hands. 'Whatever.'

'No.' She joined him. 'It's not "whatever". Just not now.'

They both reached for the same paper towel, ripping it in half. Jackson grabbed another, his jaw taut. 'You talking about our talk, or us? I knew I shouldn't have said it. I knew you'd do this.'

'Do what?' she countered. 'You told me you want to get married in a text. I deserve a minute to process it!'

'You're not processing it, Luce. You know how I feel. You've known for a while, and I know you feel the same. You're just going to use this to push me away. I'm not demanding we do it tomorrow, but it is something I want. I thought you might too.'

He dropped the used towels in the bin, and she blocked his exit.

'That kid, in there?' She dropped her voice. 'His mother waved him out of the door and he ended up in hospital. She got a call telling her that someone she loved, someone she tried to protect and loved, was hurt, despite everything she did to keep him safe, despite everything she taught him. He knew to wear a helmet. She taught him to be safe, to look both ways when crossing the road, to chew his food. She taught him to be out in the world, and he ended up here.'

'And he's fine. He's on his way upstairs; he's alive and being looked after.' He scanned her face, his eyes widening with realisation. As usual, he saw through her shields. 'That's what this is about? Harriet and Zoe? The adoption plan?'

'It's not the adoption. I want Zoe. I like our life. I just…'

'You don't want more? I'm in this with you. I'm scared too, but we love each other, Luce. I will never not want this, want more.'

'I'm not scared.' She breathed. 'I'm terrified!' They were drawing attention now, her raised voice turning people's heads. 'I have to go, Jackson. We're at work.'

He grabbed her hand and wound his fingers around hers, grounding her frantic feet.

'I love you.' His voice was low in tone but not conviction. 'I'm here. I'm not going anywhere. Nothing has changed since this morning. I get that you're stressed. I'm sorry I didn't tell you in a better way, but I'm here—*for ever*.'

'You can't know that. Don't promise me what you don't know.'

His expression was so sad, she could barely hold his gaze.

'Oh, darling.' He squeezed her hand. 'My brave, stubborn heart. Tomorrow, I can't promise. You've got me there, but all of my todays are yours—yours and Zoe's. I will love you today and today and today, for as long as we've got. But you have to let me. You have to trust me. I want you to be my wife. I want to shout from the rooftops that I'm your husband.'

'Jackson, we have incoming!' Josh hollered, coming round the corner on fast feet. 'Sorry.' He winced, seeing them together. He looked back at Jackson. 'Two minutes out.'

'I'm coming.' Jackson dropped a kiss on her forehead. 'Think about it, Lucy.' She stared up at him blankly, stunned by his words.

He loves me. He wants me as his wife.

The second he'd said it out loud, her heart had felt it. Felt the solidity of his truth. 'I'm yours, and you are mine. Don't shut that out, not when we're this close. Love trumps tomorrow.'

With a rueful smile, he left her there, standing by the sink, motionless in a sea of busyness.

Love trumps tomorrow, he'd said. She thought about it the whole way back to the ward. She allowed herself to digest the conversation.

When I get back to the ward, that's it—back to work, snakes at the ready, shields up.

Holding her ID badge to the admission panel, she shrugged her shoulders back and held up her chin.

The letter from Harriet was in her locked desk drawer. Pulling it out, she pushed her paperwork to one side, smoothing out the pages.

She'd read it a lot over the last few months. She used it to hear her sister's voice in her head and remind herself why she was doing this. Ronnie and Harriet had known just what they were doing. She'd kicked and scratched her way through things, but they knew. It seemed everyone knew. They'd known when Ronnie had been alive, even when they'd been tearing strips off each other, when she'd declared him to be the most annoying man on the planet.

Rereading the letter for the hundredth time, she longed for her sister. She wished she could talk to her now about Jackson, about how scared she was. If Harriet were here now, she'd tell her how proud of her she was. How jealous she was of her ability to have leaped to form a family after living through the loss of their parents.

'I thought I was the brave one,' she said to the photo of Harriet sitting on her desk. 'Look at me now, eh? I know you said in your letter I'd be mad, but I'm pretty sure you're raging up there, or wherever you are.' Her pager went off; Lachlan was there. 'Oh, what does it matter?' She huffed, locking the letter back up. 'Tomorrow comes, no matter what you do. Screw today.'

Heading to Lachlan's room, she shoved her head back in the game. Taking a deep breath, she knocked and went in.

'Hi,' she said to a woman sitting next to his bed. 'Lachlan's mother, I assume?'

'Yes—Julia. His dad's just gone to get us some coffees.'

'Nice to meet you. I'm Dr Bakewell. Have you been updated?'

His mother, a small, rather worried looking woman who was the double of Lachlan, nodded back. 'The nurse said something about a scan.'

'That's right.' She looked at Lachlan. 'Your head injury has been checked over and we're satisfied it's just a concussion. Your laceration was glued in A&E, the cut on your arm has been cleaned and stitched and your nose isn't broken, but it will be very bruised and sore for a while.'

'That's it?' his mother checked. 'Nothing's wrong with his head? He knocked himself out.'

'I know, but he's fine. We'll keep him overnight to observe him, but tomorrow he should be well enough to discharge. You'll need bed rest at home, and no skate…'

His mother burst into loud sobs.

'He's really okay?' She sobbed.

'He's going to be fine,' Lucy said softly. 'We will take excellent care of him, I promise. He'll be home tomorrow.'

'Oh, God!' she cried, tears rolling down her cheeks. 'Thank you, thank you.'

'Mum…' Lachlan groaned, trying to reach for her hand. 'Don't cry!'

'I can't help it,' she managed to get out. She saw him reaching for her and clasped his hand tight between hers. 'If I wasn't so happy, I would be really mad, Lachie.'

Lucy stepped back, watching the teenager's bottom lip wobble. 'I know, Mum, I'm sorry. I swear, I'll always wear my helmet from now on.'

She kissed his hand, cradling it in hers and reaching over to brush back his hair from his face.

'You'd better, my boy. I can't function without you, okay? You're my world. I need you around.'

Lachlan sniffed. 'Love you, Mum,' he croaked.

'Love you too.' She smiled, her watery eyes bright. 'You're a pain in the bum sometimes, but I need you.'

Lachlan laughed. 'I need you too.'

'I'll…er… I'll let you have some time.' Lucy left the room, her legs shaking with every step.

I can't function without you.

Her kid hadn't worn a helmet. Something so basic, ignoring a request that could have caused a different ending—an ending she'd experienced first-hand, four times over. Watching them together in that room, so happy and elated to have escaped that, all she could think of was her people, her family: Zoe and Jackson.

For most of her life, she'd not only worn a helmet, she'd been too scared to get on her skateboard. Lachlan's mum had taken all the precautions, had had all the worry. She'd taught her son and he'd still got hurt. But she didn't regret being his mother, did she? She'd run to him, told him how important he was to her. She'd run to his side and stayed there, just as Jackson had for Lucy. No matter what she did or said, he was there, not fearing tomorrow.

She stood outside the room, heart pounding, and asked herself a question she hadn't dared ask before: if Jackson was hurt, would she regret it? Would she run to him, or run the other way?

She remembered his promise to her.

All of my todays.

For once in her life, she let the tears fall freely. Because she finally realised, no matter what happened down the road, no matter when tomorrow dawned, she loved him. If he had to leave her and this world, it wouldn't matter to her whether they were wed or not. But it would matter to him.

Lifting her tear-streaked face to the ceiling, she smiled. 'Okay, guys. You win.' She went to pull out her phone. 'It's time to get on that freaking skateboard.'

'Lucy!' Amy shouted, running down the corridor towards her as the nurses' station buzzed into life. Her pager went off in her pocket. 'Emergency!'

The warning siren went off around them and both women took off running.

CHAPTER THIRTEEN

THE SECOND LUCY got there, she knew something was really wrong.

There was a huge flurry of activity as her team gathered at the nurses' station. Her number three, Dr Adebi, was shouting orders at the rest of the staff, calling them out name by name. Once they got their instructions they rushed off, professional and nimble, eager to get on with their designated task.

'What's the emergency?' Lucy asked, running to his side. Dr Adebi turned to her once the last of the staff was sorted, but his words were half-drowned out when the lockdown alarm sounded again. An announcement asking people to stay calm and remain where they were rang out on repeat.

'We're getting reports of a man with a weapon in the hospital. A porter was injured in the back delivery bays. Security is trying to track the man down. Porter was stabbed in the stomach once, and once in the arm as he tried to stop the guy.'

'Lockdown procedures need to be initiated immediately, no one in or out.'

Dr Adebi nodded, pointing to the ward doors. 'We already locked it down, SCBU too.'

'Shutters on the windows facing the corridor?'

Dr Adebi shrugged, his eyes wide. 'I'm not one hundred percent. I told the nurses to take the children who could be moved to the day room at the end of the hall, as per your protocols. Lunch is done, so we should be able to hole up for a while.'

She patted his arm. 'Go and round on the patients, make sure all observations are carried out on time. Nothing gets missed.'

He gave her a solemn nod and got to it. She picked up the phone, checking with maternity and SCBU that everything was locked down and all people accounted for. She knew they'd already locked down A&E. She felt better, knowing Jackson was safe, somewhere close. She hoped his parents weren't seeing any of this on the news. They'd been through enough worry.

The ambulances would have been diverted to other hospitals already. The other staff were coping well, pulling together as a team. The wards worked in conjunction with each other, all following the protocols and procedures. Now all they had to do was reassure the parents, carers and patients they had with them on the ward. Heading to the TV room, she pushed down the feelings of worry she had for the hospital and its inhabitants. Ensuring her patients were calm and still getting the best care was paramount.

'Right,' she said with a broad smile, taking in the sight of children in chairs, their parents' laps and wheelchairs and closing the door behind her to help muffle the sounds outside. 'Who fancies a movie, eh? We have headphones!'

She didn't hear a thing for the next hour. All the updates were the same: no one in, no one out. All non-emergency surgeries were cancelled. One of her patients was locked down in the post-surgery recovery room after having had a hernia repaired, and young Ada's parents were distraught at not being able to be there for their cute little five-year-old. Lucy had allocated one of the healthcare assistants to keep an eye on them. She knew what it was like to wait for news, and she looked after the parents and guardians just as well as she did the children.

Amy came to find her just as she was going on her rounds again.

'Ada's fine. The OR nurses got one of the tablets. I put the parents in one of the side waiting rooms so they could talk to her in private.'

Lucy patted her hand gratefully. 'You're a star; they should feel so much better after seeing she's okay.'

'Yeah.' Amy smiled, but it didn't last. 'I'll be glad when this thing's over. I heard from one of the OR nurses that someone else has been stabbed.'

'Someone on the staff?' Lucy asked, appalled. Amy shrugged.

'I don't have the details; it was pretty hectic there. They were getting him up to Theatre; she didn't have time to stay on the line.'

'Right,' Lucy replied, pulling out her phone.

She typed out a message to Jackson at super-speed.

Are you okay?

Then she got back to work, Amy in tow.

'Hey, Nathan, how's the apocalypse going?'

Nathan was one of her older patients, at sixteen, and secretly one of her favourites.

'Not bad. I finally kicked that level's butt last night.'

'Yeah,' she teased, washing her hands in the little sink near his bed. 'The night staff told me. No wonder you look tired. Three a.m.?'

Nathan winced. 'Can't believe they grassed me up.'

'They didn't, I read it on your observation chart. My team don't sweat the small stuff, but you do need to get your rest. Can I check your sutures?'

Nathan groaned, putting his game on pause. 'Fine,' he droned. 'But...' His smile turned mis-chievous. 'Since my parents couldn't get in today, you can't tell them that I didn't do my homework yet. Deal?'

Lucy pretended to ponder his bribe. 'Is it biology?'

'No, English lit.' Lucy's eyes flicked to the small stack of paperbacks Nathan had brought with him when he'd come in for his small bowel surgery and nodded. She wouldn't have been able to concentrate in his shoes, with all the excitement going on around him. If killing some zombies distracted him from being in hospital on lockdown when he should have been at school, that was fine with her.

In a kinder world he'd have been hanging out with his mates and not dealing with Crohn's. This operation wasn't the first he'd had. He lived on a special diet and had to endure a colostomy bag. He was a happy teenager who worked hard. One bit of homework missed was hardly going to derail his life. He read in the evening; she'd seen him plenty of times. They'd even swapped books before, ones she'd loved at his age.

'Fine, deal. What do you say, Dr Ackles?'

Amy laughed as she wrote on his chart. 'A day off on doctor's orders? They can't be mad at that.'

Donning gloves, Lucy gently removed the dressings, checking over the operation site. 'Good, it's healing well. No sign of infection or swelling. The surgeon said it went well.'

Nathan smiled. 'Yeah, they managed to save more than they thought, which is good, because I am sick of seeing you guys.'

Lucy pretended to be wounded, miming the removal of an arrow from her heart. 'Ouch,' she laughed. 'Cheers, Nath. We love you too.'

'When do you think the hospital will be open for visitors?' he asked as she finished up.

'Tomorrow, I would have thought,' she said, making sure she didn't show how uncertain she was. 'You have your phone, right, to video call your parents?'

Nathan nodded. 'Yeah, I told them to stay at work. I think they were planning to stage a vigil outside at one point!' He huffed, his trademark teenage eye-roll evident. 'I heard Isaac say the police were here. They would have freaked.'

'Hey.' She laughed, getting his attention. 'Don't knock it. Believe me, having parents that care and fuss like yours do is not a bad thing. It's nice having someone that cares for you.'

One of the nurses knocked on the door and Amy went to see what they wanted. When she came back, her face was white.

'What?' Lucy asked, knowing instantly that something was wrong.

'Nothing.' She went to open the blinds she'd closed for the examination. 'Good news, actually—the lockdown is being lifted.' She let the light into the room, making Nathan squint and hiss theatrically. 'Dr Bakewell, I need a word outside, please.'

Lucy passed Nathan his controller. 'See you

later.' She followed her colleague outside. 'What's up?' she asked straight away. 'Did they get the guy?'

'Yeah.' Amy breathed. 'They got him, but you need to go to Jackson, Lucy.' She watched Amy's lips form more words, and then she was running.

Not again, her voice was screaming in her head. *Not again. Why us?*

She ran down corridor after corridor, barrelling past people, banging on doors, demanding that they let her through, screaming that the lockdown was over and to let her get past. Her phone was at her ear, but all it was doing when she called Jackson was ringing out, ringing out again and again.

Finally, she was there. Josh saw her running and came over. He took her to one side, towards Resus Two.

God, no, not that room. That was the room they'd taken her sister and Ronnie to. That room meant death.

Josh kept talking, his voice hushed, his arm around her shoulder as he laid out the details for her.

The guy with the knife had gone to A&E; he had walked right through the hospital and not been stopped. The security team had still been scrambling to get a description since the first alarm had been raised. In the chaos, he'd slipped by everyone. The loading bay doors had CCTV, but he'd been obscured by a delivery van. The bloke had walked right past people into A&E, where Jackson had been working. The lockdown between departments had still not been in full effect, the chaos still fresh. Jackson had blocked his path and challenged who he was. When he'd seen the blood on his clothes, he'd reacted.

Jackson had tried to protect everyone.

The attacker had lunged. Lucy couldn't get a breath big enough to fill her lungs as she listened, and it looked as if they were walking straight to the room she'd never wanted to set foot in again.

Not Jackson, she thought. *Not now. Please. It's not fair. Not that room.*

They were almost there, her steps slowing as Josh kept talking about how the man was in custody, how Jackson was a hero. How bad it could have been. She didn't want to hear any of that. She didn't want to hear that Jackson was a hero. He was already *her* hero. He was hurt, or worse, and life was changing again. She'd run from him, from his love, for so long. They could have had more todays. She had so much to say. She'd barely begun loving him.

Zoe… Zoe couldn't lose another person.

They were almost at the doors now, and she didn't hear or see anything else—not the lighting, not the patients or the staff, dealing with the aftermath of the last few hours. All she saw was those big wooden doors, the ones she'd pushed through half a year ago. She couldn't feel Josh's arms around her shoulders. She didn't hear him talking or see the faces they passed as she tried to put one numb body part in front of the other. Her phone was still in her hand, which was useless, because she couldn't reach whom she wanted to talk to. It was too late for him just to pick up the phone and for everything to be normal.

'I can't do this again,' she said. 'I can't. Not again.' When they passed the doors, her knees buckled. Josh took her over to a set of chairs and sat her down. He kneeled in front of her, calling a nurse to bring them some water.

It was then she truly understood. She loved him—today, tomorrow, for ever. She was completely in love with Jackson Denning. She loved him enough to run down that aisle, with him holding her hand. She'd walk through fire for him. She'd been over-the-top obsessed, to the point of losing her mind, with him since the day she'd seen the big lug howling and clutching his bruised nether regions.

He'd always been there—in the background, in her face, in her thoughts. Pushing her to be the best at work, if only to one-up him. They made each other better, and she didn't know another man walking the earth who could handle her like he could. Who could understand her and be part of her family. He was always challenging her, annoying the hell out of her. He made her feel alive, sexy. He saw her like no other did. He'd always seen her as if she was transparent under his gaze. He loved her, and she jolly well loved him too. Of course she should be his wife…in this life, in every life.

It was then she realised that Josh hadn't taken her to his side. He hadn't taken her to that room, the one she'd once barged into, looking for her sister, for Ronnie. Looking for proof that what she knew in her head wasn't true. She turned to look at the wooden barrier between Jackson and her. It was still. No one was coming or going. No one was barking orders or running in with crash trays.

'I never told him,' she said, her tears taking over. 'I know the answer now, and I'll never get to tell him. To see his stupid grin.'

'What?' Josh asked, his voice finally filtering through to her ears again. 'Lucy, I think you're in shock. Please drink this.' She pushed the cup away with a shaky hand. She felt sick and dizzy, so dizzy. Her head was spinning. She'd run again when he'd needed her. He'd spilled his guts and she'd left him hanging. It was too late. He was gone. He'd never know now.

'Lucy!' Josh boomed. 'She's passing out! Hold her head!' Arms scrambled around her as her sight turned to pinpricks, surrounded by black. 'Can we get some help here? Lucy,' she heard Josh say to her, 'we've got you.'

And then she let go and succumbed to the nothingness.

When she woke up, she was in a side cubicle in A&E, the curtains drawn around her. She sat up with a jerk when her memory slammed into action.

'Careful,' a deep voice said. Her head whipped to the side and she looked straight into Jackson's big, brown eyes. 'Take it slowly.'

He was lying in a bed next to hers, his bare chest sporting a dressing. He had a split lip, and a deep bruise was forming around his right eye.

'Jackson!' she squeaked, her voice strangled. She pulled her blanket back and went to him. He reached for her hand as she sank to the chair next to his gurney. He pulled it to his lips and kissed it, wincing when it touched his injury. 'I thought you were…were…'

She started to cry then. Relief and shock flowed out of her. He pulled her closer, his other hand coming up to grab her cheek.

'Trig, I'm fine. I'm okay, Luce.' He looked down at his chest. 'The guy stabbed me. I clocked him the second he walked in, but security was thin on the ground. He was looking for another patient. Some ridiculous gang territory thing.'

She didn't care about any of that, she just cared that he was there.

'Shh,' he soothed her. 'Don't cry, darling, please. It'll drive me crazy. I can't get to you properly like this.'

She laughed, and it sounded hysterical between the sobs.

'You're lying there and you're worried about me,' she keened, leaning forward and kissing him. He made a pained hissing sound but, when she pulled back, he leaned his head closer to keep the contact. He kissed her softly, one kiss on each corner of her mouth and the tip of her nose.

'That's how this works,' he said once he'd let her go enough to look her in the eye. 'I'm fine.' He winked at her with his good eye. 'You're not getting rid of me that easily.'

She got his double meaning, and she didn't need to think twice about anything now. She knew she would never run from this man again. Almost losing him had woken her up. Life was short and cruel. She didn't want to miss a minute of it, good or bad, light or dark.

'I love you and I want to be with you. Yes…in every single way!' she blurted. 'I panicked when you said it today. I wanted to run, but I will never do that again.'

'Luce, you don't have to say this. You don't have to pity me or feel bad.'

'I don't. I already knew the truth; I just didn't

want to face it. I thought I'd never get the chance to tell you. I thought I'd never get to say it.

'I love you. I love you, Jackson, body and soul. I swear, I would go through a lifetime of pain and lonely tomorrows for ten minutes being loved by you today. I'm sick of hiding in my half-life. I want us to be a family, a proper family. So, marry me, and yes—that's what I want to say. A question and an answer, no more time wasting.'

He didn't say anything at first. She studied his beautiful, broken face for clues.

Was she too late? What if he'd realised she wasn't worth it after all?

'Took you long enough,' his deep voice teased. 'Get in this bed, right now. I need you close.'

She scrambled in carefully, feeling the warmth of him against her. She kissed his cheek over and over when he tried to smile and whimpered at the pain it produced.

She held his face close to hers and said over and over, 'I love you…for ever.'

'Wow,' he mumbled from under her. 'I should get stabbed more often.'

'Not funny.' She scowled.

'I love you too, Luce,' he said in her ear as she held him tight. 'I always have.' His grin lit him up from the inside. 'We're getting married, Trig.'

'You bet your lanky behind we are, Sasquatch.'

EPILOGUE

Two and a half years later

'HEY!' JACKSON MET them at the front door, taking her shopping bags out of her hands as he always did. They walked down the hall to the kitchen and he leaned down for a kiss on the way, as if he couldn't wait any longer. 'Missed you,' he mumbled into her ear. Even after all this time, she still shivered when he did that. She still found him as hot as the day they'd met. The late August weather was fine, the sun blazing high in the sky.

'Did you get everything you needed?'

Lucy puffed her fringe out of her eyes, heading straight to the fridge to get them both a cold drink.

'We sure did, eh, doodlebug?'

Zoe was trying to get up on one of the stools on the island, her face like thunder.

'Mummy made me go to loads of shops. It was so boring.' Jackson lifted her up, making her laugh as he blew raspberries on her cheek.

'Oh, no, not shopping!' he teased. 'Did you get your school uniform?'

'Yes.' She grinned, brushing her blonde hair

back with a little hand and reaching for the juice Lucy had put on the counter. She slurped when she drank, her eyes on the back door. 'Can I play outside now?'

Lucy was busy unpacking groceries from one of the bags. 'Till lunch, of course.'

'Yes!' Zoe punched the air, and it immediately reminded Lucy of Jackson. She was a Mini Me of him, all guns blazing, just like him. She wasn't one for shying away from things, and it thrilled Lucy to see it.

Jackson caught her mid-air as she shuffled off the stool, brandishing sun spray.

'Aww, Daddy!'

He laughed, putting her on her feet and getting down to her level to spray the sunscreen onto her skin.

'Aww, Daddy, nothing. It's hotter than Hades out there, and you're built like a child of the corn.'

'A what?' she asked, her little nose scrunching up in confusion as he lathered her up.

'Nothing. Have fun.' He dropped a kiss on her forehead and Zoe took off for the garden.

Just before she barrelled out to the swings she loved, she turned back to them. 'Don't forget to show Daddy your surprise!' She beamed, and then they were alone.

'Surprise, eh?' he fished, coming up behind her as she put the last of the food away. He tried to peek into one of the other bags but she swatted his hand away.

'Hey!' Lucy admonished. 'I wasn't going to show you till later. She snitched a tad early.'

He came round behind her, wrapping her in his arms, nuzzling at her neck. He knew that drove her crazy. Hell, one more rub of his stubble and she'd give away all her secrets.

'That's my girl. What is it? Come on, spill.'

She pretended to be annoyed with him, but she was too excited. She didn't keep a thing from him any more, not since that day when she'd thought she'd lost him.

The last couple of years had been amazing. It had been hard work, sure, and exhausting. Somewhere along the way, they'd gone from Jack-Jack and Luby to Mummy and Daddy. Zoe knew all about her parents. Their pictures still hung in pride of place in their home. She'd heard the stories and, when she'd started calling Jackson and Lucy 'Mummy' and 'Daddy', they knew that she'd decided that for herself.

Zoe was a mix of all four of them. She had her mother's looks and soft blonde hair and Ronnie's calmness. Jackson always ribbed Lucy that Zoe had inherited her stubborn streak, and Lucy saw his loyalty and open-hearted love shine out from their little girl. It had been a journey, but she loved where they were going. Living for today, it turned out, was a hell of a lot of fun.

'Come on, wifey, show me!' Jackson had started to tickle her sides and she yelped as she jumped away from him, grabbing one of the plain bags.

'Fine!' She pretended to huff. 'Before I show you, though, promise not to freak out.'

Jackson scoffed loudly. 'Pot…kettle…?'

'Shut up!' She giggled. 'Fine.' She came to stand in front of him, holding out the bag to him. He grabbed at it, a daft look on his face, like a little boy on Christmas morning. She pressed her lips together to keep the smile off her face as she observed his confused frown.

'What…?' His voice trailed off as he unfolded the small, white cotton garment. '"My big sister is…"'

'"Awesome",' she finished. 'Zoe picked it out.'

He held it up, the bag falling out of his grasp to the kitchen floor.

'This is a onesie,' he said.

'Yep.'

'For a baby.'

'Yep.'

'You—you let Zoe buy this?' he stammered, his gorgeous face a maelstrom of emotions.

'Yep.' She smirked. 'Well, I reckoned we'd need it.' She came round the island to stand in front of him. 'You know, in a few months.' His eyes bugged as his jaw dropped. 'Freaking out?' she teased.

'We're having a baby?' His voice cracked. 'For real?'

'For real.' She laughed. 'Just our timing, too. One kid goes to school full time, and we start all over again. Are you happy?' she asked, watching him look at the little outfit in his hand as if it might vanish.

'I'm not happy,' he said, lunging forward and picking her up in his huge, muscular arms. 'I'm freaking ecstatic! Zoe!' he shouted, and she appeared at the back door. 'We're having a baby!' He yelled, twirling Lucy round on the spot.

Zoe rolled her eyes, a classic Lucy move.

'I know, silly! I'm the big sister!' She put her hands on her hips, nodding to the clothing in his arms.

Jackson and Lucy laughed out loud. 'Good point. Get over here, smarty-pants!'

Zoe ran over with a giggle, and Jackson reached down and scooped her up.

'My girls.' He grinned, showering them both with kisses. 'I love you,' he told them both. 'So much.'

'We love you more,' Lucy told him. Hugging them both to her, she wondered at how life could change so much. How tragedy could rip people apart and change them. It could alter their landscape for ever, but sometimes lead to something new and unexpected—something great that might never have made them so happy without going through the deep, dark sorrow first.

That night, with Zoe fast asleep after their busy day, and Jackson kissing her still-flat tummy before carrying her to bed with love and lust written all over his gorgeous face, she reminded herself never to forget how lucky she was. She liked to think that, wherever they were, the people they had lost would be watching and be happy for them…at peace. It gave her the strength to enjoy every moment and take the rough with the smooth. Squeeze every drop out of life and follow her gut in her personal life as well as in her career.

Months later, she proved just that to herself, and to the love of her life. As she cradled Zachary Ronnie Denning, exhausted from labour and eager to show Zoe her little brother, she didn't hesitate to enjoy every single second. He was perfect, just like Zoe. A child she'd made from love with Dr Denning, the man whom she'd once jokingly threatened to sterilise to do the women of the world a favour.

'I love you.' Jackson beamed, that grin bowling her over.

'Pack that grin up, Denning. I just had your baby. You'll make me want another just to make you do it again.'

'Deal,' he retorted, making her laugh. 'We can

fill the whole house with kids.' He looked at Zachary. 'He's amazing, isn't he? He has the Denning chin.'

She rolled her eyes at him. 'Let's hope he doesn't go paintballing and fall in love with a stubborn woman, eh?'

His low, rumbling laugh surrounded her as he hugged them both to him. 'I hope he does. I'll tell him it's the best thing his dad ever did, being shot in the groin by his mother.'

'Worth all the todays?'

He bent to kiss her just as the door opened. Zoe ran in, followed by two very excited grandparents.

'All the todays for ever,' he whispered. 'Fighting and loving you is what makes life worth living.'

'Deal?' she joked.

'Hell, yeah.' He growled. 'Bring it on, Trig.'

* * * * *

If you enjoyed this story, check out these other great reads from Rachel Dove

How to Resist Your Rival
A Midwife, Her Best Friend, Their Family
Single Mom's Mistletoe Kiss
Falling for the Village Vet

All available now!